Spring

Paths

An Anthology

eBook ISBN – 978-1-988291-27-7
Paperback ISBN – 978-1-988291-26-0

This anthology is dedicated to spring,
where writers set a course toward new beginnings,
where readers study the buds and tender shoots of writing.
Where everything is possible.

Also by the Seasonal Collective

AUTUMN PATHS

WINTER PATHS

"The deep roots
never doubt spring will come."

– Marty Rubin

"There are no wrong turnings.
Only paths we had not known we were meant to walk."
– Guy Gavriel Kay (Tigana)

Contents

Introduction

Amanda Evans and Shannon Dykens
(Partridge Island Publishing)

When we got started in 2019, our goal was not only to create a publishing house, but to support the writing community in New Brunswick.

Through our writing group, Write Now Saint John and Partridge Island Publishing, we have been able to support many authors in the local writing community.

But it wasn't until 2023 that we were able to find and help the larger writing community of New Brunswick by opening a community bookstore and hosting over 50 authors from across the province, showcasing a variety of authors and giving everyone a place where they can come to meet their fans, make new fans, and sign their books.

Through this venture, we have met so many interesting writers, many of them you will see in the pages of this anthology.

Spring

Paths

*

Juniper

By Sandra Bunting

WREN STUDIED THE BIG OLD SHED at the bottom of her property. The building was one of the features that had attracted her and her husband when they were looking for a house to buy ten years before. Potential. The structure was sound - not a sign of rot in the silvery gray boards. Inside was clean and dry with the comforting feel of wood. They had carried in a big old table and chairs, put up lanterns and in summer, sometimes wandered down with friends for a couple of beer or a bottle of wine. It wasn't quite a party place, but it created a relaxed atmosphere, amenable to getting together on a warm night. When it got cooler, they built a firepit outside to sit around and watch the ever-changing river.

Much of the couple's time was spent in the old farmhouse they were fixing up. A money pit they knew but it suited their lifestyle. They were taking their time, doing a little each year, working on a garden, trying to be more sustainable. Over time a selection of cats made their way into the house, strays attracted by the comfort and affection which permeated the home. With difficulty they made the decision to stop at five. Wren's husband Reg told her she was just a hair's breath away from becoming a crazy cat lady. The cats always stayed inside, away from the numerous birds – mostly chickadees and nuthatches – which flitted around the house's various feeders, sometimes competing with a little red squirrel or two. The first thing Wren and Reg planted were sunflowers for their cheeriness. Come August the greedy blue jays would attack the seeded centre, creating an agreeable design of blue feathers surrounded by the yellow petals.

They did up the closed-in porch during the Covid years when they were spending time exclusively in their own company due to the virus. They insulated, replaced windows, put in a propane stove and some cosy chairs. It became Wren's special place to read, sip tea and just think.

Reg used the shed as an office for his job as a graphic designer during that time. Wren still commuted to her work when she could. During the pandemic, summertime was easier for her as she worked outside, away from people.

When restrictions eased, the couple hung up lights, looped them around the shed again, and invited their friends. It felt festive, especially after the imposed isolation of quarantine and winter.

Wren thought back to the last get-together they had in summer. Their friends – four other couples – had just left. Wren and Reg remained and sat staring into the fire. She took his hand and looked into his eyes.

"I think this place is ready now for a new addition."

"We talked about that, Wren. Five cats are all we can comfortably live with."

He watched as her mouth turned into a shy smile.

"You mean, you are...?"

"No, no," she smiled. "Just that I'm ready now."

Reg hooted.

"As long as it is not another cat, or one of your ugly old moose, I'm all for it."

"Ha, ha."

They linked arms and walked dreamily back to the farmhouse along the well-worn path.

Of course, Wren didn't actually have a moose. Reg was referring to her job in the wildlife section of Natural Resources. Among her other duties, she monitored local moose population numbers, and looked at ways to improve their wellbeing. She was also working on an important project with her counterparts in Norway.

After a leave of absence, Wren walked into work. She was happy to see Trudy, the receptionist she liked, behind the desk.

"Well look who's here! Everyone will be so glad to see you back."

"I'm just popping in for a few minutes. I don't think I am ready to start work again yet. I'm here to get my laptop and some files."

"Just let us know when you are." Trudy softened her voice and looked caringly at Wren. "How are you doing anyway?"

"Better."

Wren walked down the corridor and opened the door to her office. She found everything the same as she had left it – the small adjoining lab, her books and files tidied away in a cabinet, charts on the wall. She glanced at the blown-up photos of young moose. *We all just try to survive,* she thought. Many of the baby moose were plagued by ticks, thousands of them sucking the animal's blood and life force, causing them to weaken and sometimes perish. Applying a pesticide had helped a few. Wren hoped she could save more. In a way she was monitoring ticks as well. Their numbers had been increasing significantly, another symptom of climate change. The mild winters and hot humid summers were just what the pests needed. Everything is striving to thrive.

Wren grabbed what she came for, locked her office door, and walked back to reception. She had missed the place. Her director had told her to take her time; when she was ready, she could come back.

"We need you, Wren. The moose need you. Moose have always been important to this province. But without the young ones…"

The receptionist watched her.

"Well?"

"I'm not sure. Maybe soon. I'll let everyone know when. I still want to think about it."

"I'm so sorry, Wren. Reg was a wonderful man. And so talented."

"That he was. At least he didn't suffer too long. It was quick. Seemed long, but it wasn't."

Reg had survived Covid. Ironically, while he was in hospital with it, they discovered a cancer that proved to be aggressive and untreatable. He was gone in a matter of three tortuous months.

Wren sat in the porch having tea when she heard a car drive up. Mrs. Bartley peeked out from behind lace curtains in the neighboring house. Nosey old biddy thought Wren. Always spying. The back door opened, and a voice called out.

"Don't move. I know you're in your special spot. I wouldn't like you to disturb the cat that's on your lap."

A moment later Inez poked her head into the porch. She was one of the friends that used to hang out at the shed on weekends. It was always Wren and Reg, Inez and Dave, Clarissa and Rob, Terry and Phil, Carol and Paul.

"I brought us coffee and sandwiches."

As her lawyer and friend, Inez was advising Wren on the will, and all the other things that had to be settled after Reg died suddenly during the winter. She advised Wren to think about selling the house.

"There's a lot of maintenance on an old house for one person. And you'll have to carry a big mortgage by yourself. There's a bit of life insurance coming. But you could buy a nice condo and not have to worry about anything."

"You're as bad as Mrs. Bartley. She asked me when I was going home to Ontario. I told her I *was* home. Five different people asked me that. I'll always be 'from away'. You'd think my ten years here counted for nothing."

"You don't have to leave. But selling is something to think about. It could reduce added stress."

"I can't make that decision now."

"OK, whatever you want. Listen, I was thinking. Why don't we girls pick a night and get together every week? We could try out the restaurants, have a couple of drinks. It'd be fun."

"I'm not ready to be exposed to the outside world yet. It'll be either 'I'm sorry for your loss' and I'll get sad, or 'I suppose you'll be going home.' Then I'll get angry. But why not do it here? Cook a nice meal together."

The four friends joined Wren in her kitchen on Thursday, the first of the weekly nights they decided to get together. They worked to create a gourmet dinner served on a table with a linen cloth, candles, and fine bottles of wine.

"Wren, what are you planning for that shed?"

"I thought of fixing it up a bit. Create an Air BnB. Maybe have it as an event venue. Have weddings. Joyful occasions. Why do you ask, Clarissa?"

Clarissa passed around a picture of a large stainless steel still.

"Look at this beauty I ordered from Quebec. Only I don't have room for it. I thought I could set it up in your shed, Wren. For a time. I want to make essential oils for my aromatherapy and massage business. You could all help."

They chattered enthusiastically about the project, getting more animated after several glasses of wine.

"What do you say, Wren? Can we do it here?" Clarissa pleaded. All the friends looked at Wren expectingly.

"You can use my shed. But I'm not guaranteeing that I will join you there. That I don't know."

Mrs. Bartley walked into Wren's kitchen without knocking.

"Wren, there's a man here with a delivery. He's got several big boxes. He knocked but..."

Sometimes Wren didn't want to open the door. Her friends knew to let themselves in. But Mrs. Bartley was not her friend.

"He says it's a delivery from Quebec."

Wren jumped up from her seat in the porch, a cat landing with a soft thud on the floor.

"Thanks, Mrs. Bartley. I'll take it from here."

She directed the delivery man to the shed where he piled the boxes.

Mrs. Bartley was still in Wren's kitchen when she returned.

"All sorted now, Mrs. Bartley. She held the door open for her neighbor to leave.

"It looks interesting. What did you get?"

"Just storing things for a friend."

Wren stared at the woman and kept silent until she left. She locked the door after her.

"Oh, how exciting!" said Carol. "But it came in pieces. How are we going to put it all together?"

Terry opened one of the boxes and stole a look inside.

"Come on. I'll get my tools out of the car. We'll read the instructions, check out YouTube and work together. It'll be fun."

"Fun for you, maybe. You've got an engineering degree."

"No degrees needed. It's straight forward."

Carol started removing the packaging and laying out the pieces in orderly fashion. Soon the group had it assembled after a little tinkering and consultation of the instructions and the internet.

Finally, there it stood in the middle of the shed, its silver metal gleaming and shiny.

"What now?" asked Inez.

"Now, we can read up on the process, experiment a little. And oh, I can picture all my little blue bottles filling up with fragrant oil." Clarissa was always one to show her enthusiasm.

"Look," said Terry. "We could continue to meet up every Thursday and make a meal together, and then whoever wants to, can join in to make oils.

The friends began cooking dinner and experimenting every week. However, Wren had not joined them in the shed.

Days stretched, bringing brighter mornings. Light lingered later into the evening. Rain melted most of the snow, coaxing worms to crawl out of the thawed earth and wiggle in puddles, attracting robins. But spring in the Maritimes was always deceptive. There could be frost or a surprise snowstorm at any time. Wren started a small fire in the firepit and sat looking at the ice break up in the river. Big chunks of it spun down the fast-flowing water like small icebergs. Years ago young boys used to jump from one to another for fun. A dangerous game! *Oh, it would be nice to just float away on one of them*, Wren thought, but she was brought back to reality by her mobile phone ringing. It was Clarissa.

"Wren, I have to ask you another favor. I am building a new place to make my oils. But it won't be ready 'til summer. I ordered another still, this one copper and all the way from Portugal. Can we try it out in your shed until I'm sorted?"

Wren poked the fire and looked over at the shed.

"Yes, why not?"

A short time later large boxes were again delivered and deposited in the shed. The women cooked their usual meal and then wandered down to make oils. Terry got to work on assembling the new still. Wren joined them on this occasion.

"Oh, how pretty it is! What are we going to do with this still?" asked Carol.

"Make more oils," answered Clarissa.

"Or," said Terry, "or we could make gin."

"Or," said Carol, "we could get arrested."

"No way we're doing this," said Inez. "It's illegal. With me a lawyer and Dave a policeman, it is out of the question."

"Look," said Terry. "Nobody needs to know. Dave doesn't need to know. It would just be us girls on our night out. It'd be only for our personal use."

"I hear it's legal in New Zealand, Inez," Clarissa piped in.

"C'mon, Inez," said Carol. "We wouldn't want to do it without you."

"I shouldn't even know about such things. I should cover my ears and hum. This is not New Zealand," argued Inez.

"It sounds like a fun project," Wren piped in, showing a spark of enthusiasm for the first time in a long time, the first time since she lost Reg.

Clarissa pointed out that they could have a pile of pine needles on hand to keep up the appearance of distilling for aromatherapy.

Everyone turned towards Inez, a glint in their eyes.

"OK, I'm in. But not a word – and I mean it – to anyone. Not even to our husbands."

Wren waved her hands in the air.

"Wait a minute. It's my shed. I'm the one who'd get in trouble if we get caught. So, I decide."

Clarissa stroked the smooth surface of the copper apparatus.

"It's not illegal to own a still," she said. "Just look at this beauty. Some people often name theirs. We have to think of a good name."

"It's up to Wren. Maybe just distilling essential oils would be safer for us. Or maybe Wren should go ahead with her renovations on the shed."

The side of Wren's lip turned up in a weak smile.

"No, let's go wild. Let's do it. I won't be doing any renovations for a while anyway."

They went home that night, each with a task to research some aspect of making gin. Wren, as a scientist, looked into the process, Clarissa the botanicals, Inez all the legal repercussions, Carole made a list of all the other equipment needed.

When they met the next Tuesday Terry told them that to make gin from scratch, they would first need to ferment alcohol out of grain, potatoes, or fruit, and then distil it to increase its strength.

"But we can speed up the process if we buy pure alcohol, dilute it, and distil it."

"Sounds complicated," said Carol.

"It isn't. We just have to figure out the formula. Clarissa, I found a place we can order ethanol. We can all chip in. But you should be the one to order it. If anyone questions it, you can say you need it for your aromatherapy practice."

The ethanol arrived before they met the following week. Wren was in charge of diluting it with water so that it would be safe to distil. They infused it with juniper berries for five days, and then started it on the journey through the still. This first process was made only with juniper berries. At other times they would add different botanicals. Citrus, peppercorns, cloves, ginger, anise, angelica, orris root, cinnamon and cardamon were some of the possibilities. They read like the stock in an old-fashioned apothecary.

With the combination of talents from Wren, a scientist, Terry, an engineer, Inez, a lawyer, Clarissa, an aromatherapist and Carole a professional knitter, the friends had the discipline to clean, sterilize, study, and follow steps with precision.

It took five hours to complete the distilling process. They chatted and sipped wine, all the while waiting for that first drop to come down. Carol set up her knitting machine and worked on a sweater while they waited. A huge cheer broke out when they saw that first one drip out, followed by a steady flow of droplets.

Wren went back to work. It was a busy time as moose calves were plentiful in spring. Much of Wren's work was in the woods, which suited her. Besides her fieldwork, she was working together with the Norwegian Ministry of Agriculture and Food, the agency that dealt with moose management. She was doing research on a disease called CWD that was decimating the moose population in Norway. Chronic Wasting Disease is similar to BSE in cattle or CJD in humans. It causes weight loss, stumbling, listlessness, and other neurological symptoms. There was no cure or vaccine. The time difference between Norway and Atlantic Canada is five hours. Several days a week Wren would struggle out of bed at an ungodly hour, throw on some clothes, make a quick coffee and sit down to share findings and ideas with Lars. So far it was a factfinding project, but they hoped to attract funding to concentrate on either a cure or a vaccine. Wren was engrossed in her work. She hated to see animals suffer – especially those as majestic as the moose. It was a challenge and Wren loved a puzzle. She loved to find solutions. The work was also helping her with her grief. The work with Lars and being out in the woods made her stay in the present and kept her from fixating on her loss.

Distillation is a continuous process as the alcohol dripping out the end actually changes throughout the procedure. The liquid is not safe or good to drink at every stage and bits of it should be discarded. However, it is easier when ready-made ethanol is used. After extracting the heart from their experiment, the friends were ready to try a sip to judge the quality of their alcohol.

"Who's going first?" asked Carol. She poured their newly distilled gin into a small beaker. It was time to test it for the first time.

"I will," said Clarissa.

She took the glass vessel and took a tentative sip.

"I hope it doesn't blind me."

She took another sip.

"It's really good," she said.

The others poured themselves a tiny glass and were happy with their success.

As the weeks went by, Carol finished seven sweaters and ten hats on her knitting machine to be sold in her woollen shop. The friends got the technique of making gin and all its accents to a tee. Sessions always ended on a merry note as they tasted their wares. Wren seemed to enjoy the activity and the company of her friends, but she was always quiet during this time. There was a distance to her. Her friends did little things to boost Wren's mood. Clarissa regularly gave her a healing massage, Carol knit her a bright sweater, Terry played her a tune on the ukulele she was learning, and Inez advised her on the many things she had to deal with as a young widow.

Real warmth was finally starting to shine down. Green spears of small shoots pushed up through the earth and tree buds burst from small twigs and branches. Thoughts turned to planting and gardens.

"I have no interest this year," said Wren.

"Oh, but you have to keep up with your magnificent sunflowers."

"Yes, maybe those. The giant ones."

The friends gained an expertise in the making of gin, experimenting with different botanicals over the weeks. An individual session produced only a few bottles, so they drank a bit, and each took a bottle home.

One time as they were finishing up their gathering for the night, Carol undid her sweater from the knitting machine while the rest finished getting the gin bottled and labelled, and started to clean and disinfect the still, when they heard a knock on the door. They froze.

"Don't answer it," whispered Inez.

They stopped what they were doing and looked at each other in silent panic.

The knocking stopped and they heaved a collective sigh of relief.

But soon after there was a knock at the window, and a face looking in. Although bathed in shadow, Wren knew exactly who it was.

"Hello, Mrs. Bartley."

"Oh hello, Wren dear. I just baked some biscuits and thought that you girls would enjoy them."

"Thank you, Mrs. Bartley, but I'm afraid we are working here now."

The woman tried to peer more closely into the shed.

"Oh, OK. I just noticed you all down here every week and thought you might want a little lunch."

"If you leave them on the step back at the house, I'm sure we will enjoy them. But now we are making oils for Clarissa's aromatherapy and massage clinic. It is a sterile area."

"OK. I'll leave them there."

"Thank you, Mrs. Bartley. We will be hungry when we finish, and I'm sure they are exceptionally good."

"Good night, girls."

Everyone held their breath until she left. Then there was an explosion of nervous laughter.

Inez held up her hands.

"Right. That means it's time to stop. I am out of here."

"I'm sure she meant well." said Clarissa.

"She's probably lonely and just wanted some company."

But Inez shook her head.

"You know yourselves she's a busybody and a gossip. I can't take the risk. If anyone asks, I was never here."

"We can't stop now," said Carol. "It's just too much fun."

"Well, you can have your fun without me."

The weekly sessions continued without Inez, although she continued to visit Wren in her house.

"Wren, have you thought any more about what you are going to do?"

"With the shed? Probably turn it into an event venue. Weddings, happy occasions. I want joy in my life."

"I don't just mean the shed. Your life. How are you going to manage it all? I know I am sounding like a broken record, but you could be happier if things were simple. Not a house with a lot of maintenance and a project that would take a lot of work. You love your job. You wouldn't have time for both."

Wren nodded.

"I know you're probably right, Inez. It's just so hard to let it go."

As late spring turned into early summer, the flowers Clarissa had been waiting for were finally blooming.

"We can take a rest from making gin," she told them. "And now make tinctures and essential oils with all these sumptuous blossoms."

Wren cleared her throat.

"I guess it's time to tell you. It has been fun, but Clarissa, you will have to find another place for your still. I have decided to sell the place."

"But you love it here."

"Yes, I do. But it's time to make a move. I have an offer to work in Norway. We got our funding to do research into moose diseases. Our findings could help the moose here too, everywhere really. I have a leave of absence for two years, and then I will take it from there. I told them today I'll accept. I'll pack up everything, and Inez will handle the sale of the house."

Wren set out some glasses and took down a bottle of a particularly good batch, poured everyone a glass, and made a toast.

"I'll miss you. Thanks for being with me at this time. I know I wasn't at my best". She raised her glass. "To the importance of friendship and of getting together to do something worthwhile. Like making gin."

They savored the bright, zesty taste.

"And here's to Wren's special shed and the juniper path that always leads us to where we are meant to be going."

"I'll drink to that," they shouted.

They walked out of the shed, closed the door and ambled arm in arm up the path away from the river, lively now and free of ice, dressed in almost summer blue, and flowing out to the bay. About halfway up the path, they heard a rustle in a wooded area off to the right, and tentatively looked through the foliage to discover a moose and her tiny calf calmly nibbling new buds and a few leaves that had unfurled. The mother moose lifted her head and looked directly at Wren with her large brown eyes. She seemed to nod before she turned to led her little one further into the bushes and off in the direction of the river.

Sandra Bunting

Sandra Bunting's publications include two books of short fiction, two poetry collections, a non-fiction book besides articles, poems and stories in numerous literary magazines. Sandra is on the editorial board of the Irish-based literary magazine, *Crannóg*, and worked at NUI Galway where she set up the Academic Writing Centre and taught Creative Writing and TEFL teacher training. Now living in Atlantic Canada, she is a member of *The Writers Union of Canada*, *New Brunswick Writers Federation*, *Words on Water Miramichi*, the Grand Barachois group *Women Who Write* and the *Galway Writers' Workshop*.

www.sandbunting.com

The Old Belfries Farmhouse

By Pierre C. Arseneault

VIVIAN, HER HAIR TIED IN A SHORT PONYTAIL that once was blonde but now mostly gray, wiped at the countertop, her strong arms flexing like she was trying to remove the varnish.

"Another coffee?" Vivian asked scrawny old Francis, the only person occupying one of the four barstools in the dimly lit bar.

Francis, a battered old paperback copy of *The Shining* in his hand, flushed as Vivian caught him looking at her jiggling bosom as she wiped at the sticky surface of the bar.

"Not if I want to sleep tonight," Francis answered, adjusting his dirty ball cap, scratching his stubbly chin, and pushing his near empty cup away.

"What about you folks?" Vivian said to her only other patrons, a young couple sitting at a table near the bar. "You be wanting any more coffee?"

"We're good," the brown-haired woman in the wrinkled yellow t-shirt and jeans said.

"You sure?" Vivian asked again. "Even if it's free? I'm just gonna dump it out if nobody wants it."

The man in the black *Twilight Zone* t-shirt and beige cargo shorts, the woman's husband Vivian assumed, shook his head no.

Vivian glanced at the clock. Francis would stay a while longer, looking to chat about politics and ending up on the topic of how cheap imports killed his electronics repair business just before he could retire, like he often did. This new couple though, she'd never seen them before.

Hudson's Bar and Grill wasn't quite what it used to be. People didn't hang out in bars the way they used to back when they'd opened in the mid 80's. Now they stayed home and watched Netflix, streaming the newest obsession as fast as they could, gorging on potato chips. Something else Francis griped about regularly, she thought. Mostly people came to Hudson's for the food and by eight in the evening, the place was usually deserted.

"I hope you weren't planning on ordering any more food. The kitchen closed an hour ago, the cook went home, and you don't want me cooking anything for you unless you like it burnt," Vivian stated with a sly smile.

"Amen to that," Francis muttered.

"We already ate," the man said glancing at the stack of dirty dishes on the table before them. Vivian took this as a hint that she should have cleared their table already. She grabbed a gray square plastic tub and walked over.

"You folks just passing through?" Vivian asked the strangers while collecting the dirty dishes into her bin.

"We bought a house up the way," the woman in the yellow t-shirt said.

Vivian paused, a dirty plate in hand, her thumb in a smear of gravy as she spoke.

"The old Belfries farmhouse with the old barn in back?" Vivian inquired. Her assumption based on that being one of the only houses for sale in the area.

"The old barn with the rusted metal roof," the woman in the yellow t-shirt added.

"That's the one," the man said, smiling what looked like a forced smile, Vivian thought.

"Well, I'll be," Vivian said, smiling in return. "That makes us neighbors," she said, putting the plate in her bin, wiping gravy on her beige blouse, and extending her hand out for a friendly neighborly shake.

"The name's Vivian Hudson. I own the place now that my husband's gone and died on me. I live next door to you. Well, about a little over a mile down the road away from town, which is the closest thing you have for a neighbor, where you're at."

"Anthony Gilmer," the man said, shaking Vivian's hand. "This is my wife, Melinda."

"Pleased to meet you," Vivian said, shaking Melinda's hand with gusto. "I'd heard the old house sold. I was wondering who finally bought the place."

"That would be us," Anthony said, glancing at his wife.

"Did you hear that, Francis? The Gilmer's here bought Wesley's old place."

Francis set down the paperback, pivoted on his stool and looked at the couple before turning back to his book.

Melinda tugged at her t-shirt and shifted in her chair as she spoke.

"Mind if I ask you a question?" she said to Vivian.

"Sure," Vivian replied with a smile as she set the bin down on the edge of the table and finished clearing the dishes. She couldn't help but notice the woman seemed uncomfortable now. "Ask away. We're neighbors after all."

"We thought the owner, this Mister Belfries had passed away. Which is why the house was repossessed and sold to pay back taxes or something."

"From what I can tell, the real estate agent probably didn't really tell us everything," Anthony added.

"Oh dear," Vivian replied. "They didn't tell you, did they?"

"That explains why the house finally sold," Francis said from his seat at the bar, still sitting with his back to the table. He dog-eared the page he was at like a monster and set the book down.

"A lady at the hardware store said she hoped we find the bodies so the townsfolk could have closure," Melinda said, a serious look on her face as she spoke.

"Well, you don't gotta worry about that none," Francis stated. "There ain't no bodies to be found."

Vivian frowned, picked up her bin of dishes and returned behind the bar.

"You want to tell it?" Vivian asked, looking at Francis as she spoke.

"Buy me a beer and I'll tell it," Francis replied to Vivian. "I'm gonna need more than just coffee to tell them about the Belfries house."

"Make that three beers, on us," Anthony said twirling a finger in a circle to indicate himself, his wife and Francis.

Francis got up off the barstool leaving his paperback where it lay, hitched up his raggedy jeans that seemed too big for him even though he wore a distressed looking leather belt. Strapped to the belt were a multitool and battered flashlight, both in worn leather holsters. He strolled to the table and with a scrawny, veiny arm, grasped a chair from the nearest table and dragged it over. Standing next to the chair, he spoke while glancing back and forth between the husband and wife.

"Before I tell you about Wesley and Estelle Belfries, I gotta ask. Is it too late to back out of the deal?"

"It's just a beer," Anthony started.

"Not the beer. I mean buying the house?" Francis asked.

"The deal is done, house closed last week on the first day of spring and the moving truck comes the day after tomorrow," Anthony said, glancing uncomfortably at his wife.

Francis sat down, took his ball cap off and hung it on the back of his chair. He ran his hands through his thin graying hair as Vivian placed three beers on the table, a fourth she kept for herself.

"Mind if I sit too?" Vivian asked as she pivoted a chair at the next table and sat down facing them, not waiting for their approval.

"Please do," Melinda replied, even if the bartender had already sat. "It's your bar, after all."

Francis picked up his beer, tipped it back and drank half before setting the bottle down again.

"First I need to tell you that I wasn't there for all of this and can't guarantee that everything I'm about to tell you really happened."

"Enough with the disclaimer bullshit," Vivian blurted. "Hurry up and get to the good parts."

Francis rolled his eyes and turned to Vivian. "You want to tell it?"

Vivian flicked her empty hand gesturing for Francis to continue.

Francis leaned back in his chair as he spoke.

"Well first I have to tell you about Estelle, Wesley's wife," Francis said, glancing back at Vivian to see her expression. It was always a look of awe, every time he told this story to anyone that would listen.

"She was last seen eight years ago. She'd gone down to the bingo hall with friends."

"What happened to her?" Melinda asked impatiently.

"According to Wesley, she was abducted by aliens."

Anthony smiled as his wife Melinda shot him an annoyed glance.

"And here I was thinking you were going to tell me the house was haunted," Anthony said, slugging back from his beer and setting the bottle down a bit too hard, making it foam a little.

Francis smiled, showing yellowed teeth in bad need of a dentist.

"Nothing crazy like that," he replied. "Although Wesley did imply, they thought it was at first. Because of the nightly visits and all."

Melinda smiled, blushing.

Francis knew he was embarrassing the young couple. But the lady at the grocery store, probably Grace Leblanc, said the thing about finding the bodies, making the young couple think the house might have been the scene of a grisly murder or something. A murder where they'd made the bodies disappear, Francis thought before continuing.

"Wesley Belfries asked me once if I believed in aliens," Francis said, his expression serious. "I thought he was kidding until he said they'd taken his wife."

"You're skipping ahead too much," Vivian said, leaning in and swatting Francis on the arm.

"I suppose I am. The first time I met Wesley Belfries, he came to my shop to get his VCR fixed," Francis said before pausing, leaning forward, and asking the young couple a question he often did in this scenario. "You know what a VCR is, right? A videocassette Recorder?"

Anthony's brow furrowed at first. "Oh, you're serious," he replied, now smiling. "Of course, we know what a VCR is. My grandparents still have one."

"Wesley still had an old one. Like really old. Top loading. Early model unit." Francis sipped beer and continued. "Brought it to my shop to get it fixed. The thing had chewed up a tape and he wanted me to remove it and get it working again. He was quite disappointed when I told him I didn't think I could do that."

"Why not?" Melinda asked.

"Too old," Francis replied. "He had an early generation VCR; the pinch roller and the heads were worn-out. You couldn't get parts for those models anymore. Anyway, I offered to sell him a refurbished one. It was newer and all, but he didn't like the idea at first as he was used to his. Didn't think he could make a new one work."

"You should have sold him a DVD or Blu-ray player instead."

Francis guffawed, ignored the stupidity of what he thought Anthony had just said and pressed on.

"I told him I'd go to his house after closing, hook up the new VCR for him and show him how to use it."

"Tell the part about the tapes," Vivian interrupted.

"He asked me if I could fix the tape that had gotten all chewed up and looked pretty upset when I told him I couldn't. I said that if he bought a VCR I would throw in a couple of tapes from the previously viewed ones I had for sale. He chose two copies of the same movie: *E.T. The Extra-Terrestrial*. The same movie that had gotten stuck in his old machine, turns out."

Melinda frowned, sipped beer and spoke.

"You let him take two copies of the same movie?"

Ignoring the question, Francis continued.

"So I went to his house that night, to hook up his new VCR. He had an old floor model television. Someone had already hooked up a matching transformer, so I used a coaxial cable to hook it up. The old TV didn't even have a remote, so I sat with him and showed him how to use the new VCR and we got to chatting. That's when he asked me if I believed in aliens. I assumed he'd asked because we were watching *E.T.*"

"Where was his wife during all this?" Melinda asked, leaning back and scooting down in her chair while sipping beer.

"She'd already been taken two years prior," Vivian interjected.

Francis shot Vivian a dirty look and continued.

"The place had a smell. Not like a corpse was rotting in the walls or anything. But it had an old people smell. Like a combination of RUB·A535 and tea bags left out to dry. So, I asked him that question. Where was his wife? Nobody'd seen her in two years, and he'd never reported her missing or anything. Of course, I didn't know that at the time."

"Did they have any kids?" Melinda asked.

"They'd had a son, William. He died long ago, in a car accident on his graduation night," Francis replied.

"How terrible," Melinda whispered.

"They were drunk, and William was driving so he got blamed for it all. The Belfries took it hard," Francis added. "Anyway, I remember Wesley getting choked up when he told me they'd taken his wife. I remember the shock I felt, like it was yesterday, watching an old man tear up telling me someone took his wife. It made me uncomfortable, and I remember excusing myself to go use the bathroom. I wanted to get up and leave right then and there."

"Why would you want to leave?" Melinda asked.

"Because I didn't know what to say. And I was afraid of what he would tell me next. Maybe he'd killed her and was trying to cover it up. But instead, I used the bathroom. I remember seeing her pink hairbrush with long gray hairs stuck to it, still on the sink, probably exactly where'd she'd left it. I remember while walking back to the living room; I looked in the bedroom. The bed hadn't been slept in for a long time and there was a flower print dress laid out on the bed for her."

"How'd you know the bed hadn't been slept in?" Anthony asked, his voice sounding as if he'd found a plot hole in Francis's story or something.

"Everything in there had a layer of dust on it, like no one had even been in the room in a long-long time."

Francis paused, sank the rest of his beer, set down the empty bottle and cleared his throat.

"When I went back into the living room, Wesley was watching *E.T.* with the sound off. He said he'd figured out the VCR well enough. That's when he offered me coffee or tea, like nothing strange had just happened. I told him I needed to leave but he asked me to sit a while longer. To talk."

"Did you?" Melinda asked before finishing her beer and gesturing to Vivian that she would like another. "Bring Francis another one too, please," she said.

"Wesley told me that two years before, on August fourth, he and his wife saw lights in the sky. They were in bed and only saw flashes through the blinds. They assumed it was lightning."

Vivian set fresh beers in front of Melinda and Francis and plopped back into her chair.

"He told me they saw flashes of light the next night too, but it was during a heat wave so they assumed it was heat lighting. But the third night it happened, Wesley made the mistake of getting up and looking outside."

"Why would you say he made a mistake?" Anthony asked before sipping beer.

"He saw strange lights in the sky," Francis said dryly.

"Probably a drone," Anthony said.

"That was years ago and to my knowledge, nobody around here had even heard of drones yet," Francis said dryly. "Anyway, a week later, Estelle was late coming home one night after bingo. He started getting worried, of course, but before he could go out looking for his wife, her car pulled onto the driveway. He said when she came in, she was acting strange. When he asked her where she'd been, she acted puzzled. Like she didn't know what he was talking about. She'd left bingo and came straight home."

"I'd have thought she was having an affair, myself," Vivian said, making Anthony grin. In turn making Melinda shoot her husband a cold stare.

"He knew this wasn't true. She'd been over an hour late, but she seemed her usual self. Actually, I think I remember Wesley saying she was acting all happy, even if she hadn't won anything at bingo that night."

Francis picked up his fresh beer and took a drink.

"Wesley said that night they saw the lights in the window again. This time his wife wouldn't let him get up. She'd insisted he stay in bed and that it was nothing to worry about. They didn't see any more lights until a week later. Wesley woke up at around midnight with a strange feeling that something was off and noticed his wife wasn't in bed. He got up to check on her, expecting to find her in the bathroom but she wasn't there. I remember when he told me this part," Francis said, his voice wavering with emotion. "I remember Wesley getting a little emotional and saying that somehow, he knew where she was. It was like he could feel her presence. He went out to the veranda, and he saw her at the edge of the property. She was barefoot and still in her nightgown."

Francis heard Melinda gasp while Anthony still looked skeptical but was listening intensely.

"I love this part," Vivian blurted earning herself a dirty look from Francis.

"Wesley said he called out to her, but she walked into the brush at the edge of their property. In his pajamas and slippers, he went after her," Francis said, trying not to show that a part of him enjoyed telling this story. "He couldn't run on account of the arthritis in his knees and all. He shouted at her but she either ignored him or couldn't hear him. He was the one who needed the hearing aids, not she, Wesley told me that night. Anyway, he said that when he walked out of the brush and into the clearing with the old apple trees, she was standing there, looking up. She had her arms outstretched, he'd said. It was a calm night, but he could see her hair and nightgown flapping in what looked to be a strong wind. Above her there was a dark spot in the sky. It was as if it was darker than the night sky. Wesley used the words, 'a pitch-black thing in the sky above her'. And then bright lights flashed so bright he couldn't see anything and when the lights faded, Estelle and the black spot were gone."

Francis's hand shook a little when he sipped beer.

"Wesley told me he waited there for hours, calling out to her and crying. Then at about three or four in the morning, the ache in his hips and legs was too much to bear, he went back to the house. He said he sat in his recliner, trying to ease the pain in his back, hips and legs and fell asleep. Wesley said he always dreamt but not that night. That night he didn't dream at all. And when he woke, he knew his wife was gone. But for some reason, he knew she would return to him."

"How would he know that?" Melinda asked.

"I asked him the same thing," Francis replied.

"What did he say?" Anthony asked.

"He didn't know how he knew, just that he knew. He also knew that she would return at eleven-fifty-seven PM exactly. He couldn't explain how he knew, and he understood it didn't make sense. But Estelle was okay, and she would come back. So, the next day, he laid out her dress for church on Sunday and went about his day."

Melinda sniffled, getting emotional when a box of tissues was thrust in front of her by Vivian who was also dabbing at her own eyes.

"That's when he asked me again, if I believed in aliens?" Francis said.

"What did you tell him?" Anthony asked.

"I think I said yes, but I can't recall for sure. I was dumbfounded by what he'd just told me," Francis said.

"I can imagine," Melinda muttered.

"Anyway, Wesley Belfries walked to that clearing, rain or shine, every night for almost four years. He wore a path in his lawn, into the brush and down to the clearing with the old apple trees."

"What does this have to do with a VCR?" Anthony asked.

"Typical male," Melinda blurted, her voice cracking with emotion.

"Well Wesley, while convinced his wife was okay, needed some comforting. He dug out an old copy of *E.T. The Extra-Terrestrial*."

"I love that movie," Melinda muttered.

"Me too," Vivian blurted out, blowing her nose loudly.

"*Close Encounters* is way better," Anthony said.

Vivian and Melinda exchanged a look that Francis read as unbelieving of what Anthony had just said.

"Well, turns out Wesley watched that movie every night. He'd sit in his recliner and watch E.T. and Elliott become friends."

"Every night?" Melinda asked.

"All he had was an antenna hooked to his old TV so yes. He didn't have very many options that I know of. So, every night he watched *E.T.* until his VCR ate the tape," Francis added.

"Ah," Anthony piped in. "That's where you come in."

"Yes," Francis replied.

"It's a good story," Anthony stated.

"Don't be rude, Anthony," Melinda said. "Please go on, Francis."

"While Wesley said he somehow knew his wife was okay, watching a movie about a friendly alien made him feel better about it. So, he watched the movie night after night. He'd always fall asleep in the recliner and wake up in time to walk out to the clearing and wait. Rain, snow, hail or whatever, it didn't matter. Every night he walked that beaten path to the clearing and waited. At eleven-fifty-eight he'd go home, sit in the recliner again and watch *E.T.* until he fell asleep. So, when his VCR ate his tape, he came to see me. I'd fixed a few things for him before, so he knew me."

"Okay, serious question here," Anthony said, getting a dirty look from his wife. "If this is all true and his wife hadn't been seen in what, two years? Why didn't the cops come and look into it? How could an old woman simply vanish, and the entire town not start a search party?"

"The Belfries were private people, more so after their son died. Sure, Estelle went to bingo when she was feeling up to it. But there were stretches of time when she didn't go."

"It wasn't abnormal for her to miss a few weeks, even a few months," Vivian added, nodding while she spoke.

"Anyway, just so you know," Francis said, looking at Anthony. "I was skeptical about all this too."

"How so?" Melinda asked.

"I snuck out there, many times over the years. I'd park my truck up the road and walk through the woods. I hid there, many nights, watching Wesley walk out into the clearing. Some nights, the old man picked wildflowers for his wife."

"How sweet and sad all at the same time," Melinda said.

Anthony cleared his throat and wiped away a tear, obviously trying to conceal the emotion he'd felt.

"What did you do?" Anthony asked.

"Nothing. I mean what could I do? Maybe he was delusional or something, about his wife and all. But otherwise, the man seemed okay. He never told anyone else about her being gone. He told them she was feeling ill, when they'd ask. He kept it all pretty quiet. I went to check on him about a month after I'd hooked up his new VCR. He seemed okay but it was obvious he regretted telling me about it all."

"So, you just believed his weird story about aliens taking his wife?" Anthony inquired.

Francis pointed to Anthony's *Twilight Zone* t-shirt and smiled a little.

"Wouldn't you believe him?" Francis asked.

Anthony flushed at the question.

"Look, I understand why you would say that. I had all kinds of crazy ideas," Francis said. "I mean the woman could have had a rapid decline into senility and just wandered off into the woods and died of exposure. Maybe Wesley was telling himself all this to make himself feel better about it all. Maybe it was just his way of coping."

"Exactly," Anthony replied, waving his arms triumphantly as if he'd solved it, Francis thought.

"I have to admit, on some of those days when I went out there, I did walk around the property. I looked around in the woods around the property because I had my doubts too."

"You never told me that," Vivian said.

"I've told this story to some but not a lot. Most people either believe it or none of it. But it's no secret. The story has since spread around town over the years. Most people don't know what happened to the Belfries, but there are rumors. Some say they wandered off into the woods and died of exposure."

Anthony and his wife exchanged a glance at this.

"Which is why most figure it a matter of time before the bodies are found," Francis said before sinking what was left of his second beer.

"What do you think really happened, Francis?" Melinda asked. "You were there? You talked to Wesley. Do you think he was lying or maybe delusional?"

"I did at first. But after a while, I started wondering if he wasn't telling me the truth. You see, there were a few other people who'd also seen lights in the sky. Some thought like you," Francis said looking at Anthony. "Drones or something else like that. But the last time I went out there, Wesley wasn't home, but his old Ford was. I found a slipper in the clearing, near the apple tree. No one has seen Wesley or his wife since. But something tells me they'll turn up someday," Francis said as he put his hat on.

"Dead or alive?" Anthony asked before sinking what was left of his beer.

"I don't know. Maybe neither. But I've got this strange feeling about it."

"I need to pee," Melinda said.

"Me too," Vivian added as both ladies headed to the bathroom together.

"Thanks for the entertaining history of our new house. That and creeping out my wife on our first night sleeping in the place," Anthony said as he got up from the table, digging out cash from his wallet to pay the bill.

"We thought you should know, considering you bought the place," Francis said as they waited for the ladies to return.

Anthony and Melinda didn't talk to each other again until they were alone in their vehicle.

"How much of that do you think is horseshit?" Anthony asked as he pulled their Jeep Cherokee out of the parking lot and onto the road towards their recently purchased home.

"Hopefully all of it," Melinda replied. "But from what that lady at the grocery store said, Wesley and Estelle really did go missing."

"I knew the house taxes hadn't been paid in years and that's why the house ended up on the market, but I didn't know the owners had just disappeared."

"I supposed it's not like they can add that to the listing of the house. House for sale! Previous owners may or may not come back after being abducted by aliens," Melinda said with a smile and giggle.

Anthony guffawed.

"I ever tell you how much I love your sense of humor," he said smiling at his wife.

"You realize if this was one of your *Twilight Zone* episodes, we would get a visit from aliens tonight."

Anthony gave her his classic raised eyebrow glance that meant she was on to something.

"You'd wake up in the night and I would be gone, abducted by aliens," Melinda said.

"Not anymore. Now every story needs a strong female lead, so I'd be the one getting abducted and not you."

Melinda laughed. "Getting probed on the mothership, waiting for me to rescue you?"

Anthony smiled wide as he drove.

"Something like that, yes," he said.

An hour later, Melinda was done setting up an air mattress in the upstairs bedroom. The makeshift bed they used for previous camping trips would have to do while the real bed was still in the back of a moving truck. They could treat the first few days like indoor camping, she'd said, trying to make the best of it. We'll pack only what we need, had been the conversation. Which is why Anthony insisted on bringing his old television which she could hear him cursing at downstairs.

A sudden spooky memory of the tale Francis had told them about this house and its former owners had her taking the stairs two by two. Once at the bottom, she paused on her way to the living room and stood in front of the downstairs bedroom.

"According to Francis's story, this must have been their bedroom," Melinda said.

"I assume maybe the upstairs bedroom was their son's," Anthony replied from the living room.

"Are you still tinkering with that thing?"

"I found the power cord after all. And the moving truck won't be here for another two days, in case you'd forgotten," Anthony lamented while making sure the thing was solid, propped on top of a few dusty old milk crates he'd found in the barn. "If my insomnia kicks in tonight, I want to be able to watch TV."

"The internet won't be hooked up for another week, so you won't be able to stream anything. And you didn't bring your DVD and Blu-ray collection or the player. Hooking up the TV won't be worth anything."

Anthony smiled and pulled a flash drive from his pocket.

"I packed light," referring to his extra portable copy of his favorite classic TV show.

"Had I known about your infatuation with that stupid *Twilight Zone* when we met," Melinda quipped, smiling.

"The early classics are the best. Plus, it's better than that *Friends* show you love so much," he muttered as he plugged in a surge protector strip and the television.

Melinda laughed as she went to the Jeep to fetch their camping chairs. After setting up both chairs in the living room she went back to fetch their cooler and heard her husband curse aloud.

"What's wrong?" she asked setting the cooler down on the hardwood floor.

"Damn! I brought the wrong flash drive."

Melinda dropped into a folding chair which reeked of beer from their last camping trip, reached into the cooler and grabbed a bottle of water.

"We'll go into town tomorrow and buy a new TV and Blu-ray player like you planned. You said you wanted to get a new TV anyway, right? This one must be a whopping five years old now," Melinda said, rolling her eyes.

"Eight," Anthony replied, standing back, looking disappointedly at the useless television he'd just set up. "I got it when I moved out of my parent's place."

"Maybe you'll sleep good tonight and won't need it."

"I wish. But with the move, the new job and all this change, you know very well I won't be getting much sleep tonight."

"You're forgetting about the alien visitation," Melinda joked, a sly grin returning.

"Har-har," Anthony snarked in reply.

"What's that?" Melinda asked, pointing at something in the corner of the room.

There was a small black thing protruding from the floor, against the baseboard.

"That looks like the end of an old coaxial cable," Anthony said as he grabbed the tip and pulled slowly. The cable slid from the hole making a scrapping sound in the process. "Which is connected to an old antenna wire via a converter of some sort," he added.

"Isn't there an old antenna on the roof?"

"I think so," Anthony replied as he pulled the wire more and realized it would reach the back of his television. Shrugging, he connected the wire.

"Do stations still broadcast like in the old days of antennas?" Melinda asked.

"I think so, but it's probably just local stations," Anthony replied pulling the remote from his cargo shorts pocket. He sat down in the camping chair and turned on the television to find it had a fuzzy picture.

"Looks like something is out there... in the twilight zone!" Melinda joked.

"You love it," Anthony replied as he got up, wriggled the antenna wire a bit and stood back. The picture was a bit clearer now, so he sat down.

"Is that?" Melinda asked.

"*E.T.*" Anthony replied.

"No way!"

"This is the part with the bike chase," Anthony said.

"That's just too creepy for me," Melinda said while yawning. "I can't watch that, not after everything Francis told us about Wesley and his wife Ester."

"Estelle. Wesley and his wife Estelle."

"Whatever. I'm going to bed. Are you coming?"

"Yes. I'd like to get a few hours sleep before I get abducted," Anthony replied, turning off the television and then yawned wide.

"And probed," Melinda added with a furrowed brow as she waited for her husband at the bottom of the stairs.

Anthony smiled, taking his wife by the hand as she led him up the stairs for their first night's sleep in their new home.

Ten minutes later, the young couple were asleep snuggled on their air mattress on the floor of their new bedroom, Anthony snoring loudly and Melinda's ears already stuffed with cotton as they slept.

The house looked extra dark for some reason, thought Francis as he stood at the edge of the property. Looking up above the old Belfries house, he saw a clear night sky full of stars which seemed brighter than usual. The Grand Cherokee he'd seen the young couple in was parked in the driveway.

He plucked his flashlight from its holster, flicked it on and walked to the edge of the property where there were still signs of the old path Wesley had beaten. He paused and looked back towards the house. It was still dark, but something didn't feel right. He'd have to come back during the day and wander around in the back of the property, he thought. But right now, the urge to return to the clearing and see where Wesley said his wife was abducted was strong.

After a short walk under a calm starry night sky, Francis stood at the very spot where he had found Wesley's slipper. The same place Wesley had said his wife had been abducted. He shone his flashlight at the old apple tree which he thought looked dead, even in the dark, as if it hadn't borne fruit or leaves in years. There would be no new leaves again this spring, he pondered.

In that moment, his flashlight went dark, and a sudden gust of strong wind blew his dirty baseball cap off, rustling his clothes, hair and longish beard stubble. Looking up, Francis saw a deep dark void surrounded by bright stars. Somehow this amplified the black thing directly above him. His heart raced and he felt a sudden urge to run but his feet wouldn't move.

Sudden glaring bright lights seemed to illuminate all around and then dissipated as fast as they had come.

With Francis now gone, all that remained was his hat and a flickering flashlight lying nearby.

In the dark living room, the television came on as the remote sat unused in Anthony's empty camping chair. From upstairs, emitted the sound of synchronized snoring. The picture on the television was fuzzy at first but cleared up showing a young Elliott standing in front of a shed as he tossed a baseball into a glowing light emanating from the doorway. The ball flew from the illuminated shed door and landed at Elliott's feet, making him turn, stumble and run into the house.

The picture pixelated, grew fuzzy and when it returned into focus, from the glowing shed emerged an old man, wearing slacks, a short sleeved white shirt, suspenders and one single slipper, his other foot clad in a sock only.

"Hello?" Wesley Belfries said looking around in obvious confusion. He turned and waved a hand at the shed, making a come-on gesture. From the glow of the shed emerged a barefoot Estelle Belfries still wearing her nightgown. She took her husband's extended hand and smiled at him.

A sudden rustling sound came from Elliott's house and the old couple hurried towards the television as if they would climb through it, but instead, they disappeared off to the side of the screen.

The pixelated image on the TV faded and went dark.

Three days later, Anthony found Francis's hat near the path that led to the old, dead apple tree but would never tell his wife. He snuck it into the trash that night so she wouldn't see it, not wanting to make her worry.

The following day, Melinda found an old flashlight near the dead apple tree in the clearing. She recalled seeing one just like it in a holster, strapped to Francis' belt the day they met him at Hudson's bar. Brief terror washed over her as in that moment, she decided she could never tell her husband knowing it would feed his fear that there was something odd about their home formerly known as the old Belfries farmhouse. Later that afternoon, she snuck the flashlight into the trash when Anthony wasn't looking.

A week later, Francis Thébeau was declared missing by Vivian Hudson who hadn't heard from him in over a week. Not long after, his truck was found abandoned on a stretch of dirt road, near the old Belfries farmhouse.

Neither Melinda nor Anthony said anything about what they'd found, not even to each other.

Pierre C. Arseneault

The youngest of eleven children, Pierre C. Arseneault grew up in the small town of Rogersville, New Brunswick. As a cartoonist, Pierre was published in over a dozen newspapers. As an author, he has six titles published so far:

Dark Tales for Dark Nights (2013)
Sleepless Nights (2014)
Oakwood Island (2016)
Poplar Falls – The Death of Charlie Baker (2019)
Oakwood Island – The Awakening (2020)
Maple Springs (2022)

www.mysteriousink.ca

www.pcatoons.com

When the Spring Paths Melt

By Chuck Bowie

JON LEANED BACK ON THE ROWBOAT SEAT, his eyes cast alternately from steel grey sky to the similarly hued ribs and panels of the boat's hull. He let the craft coast where it chose — 'let it run', the rowers say — and every few moments he leaned over the side to peer into the depths. His gaze fixed on the distant horizon and he sighed. "I'd give a lot to hear a blue jay again."

He took note of the tree line a kilometer off to the south, mostly tree toppers. His grandfather had cultivated Christmas trees, and had called the highest third of overgrown trees 'tree toppers'. Jon was aware of the lack of trees; of anything, really, for a dozen kilometers in any of the other directions. The boat approached a power pole, tapped it with a gentle nudge, and the craft and crew of one lost momentum. It was time for another look over the port side and into the murk.

He hadn't attempted to slide into the water until this point in the day, and Jon did not look forward to dropping into its depths. He hadn't yet donned his wetsuit and eyed the parka under the bow deck. *A bit of overkill for the weather, but it'll warm me up once I come out of that water.* He grabbed a guy wire which was attached to the nearest pole, and pulled the boat over to a fifty-meter grey shadow that ran an arm's length under the water. A roofline.

Which roof? Jon tried to picture the Prospect Street architecture, but it had been a month (two months?) since he'd walked its length, and even then it had been in hip waders. He studied the power poles, noting the second and third storeys of the few buildings that were visible. A picture began to form, suggesting the street itself, and he could then draw an image of where each building could be found beneath the glossy wet surface. Now, which one housed the convenience store?

His headphones fed him a steady diet of Elliott Smith. He'd listened exclusively to Smith for almost a week. *Was it a week? A month? Since yesterday? Does time really fly? Is the concept of time an acceptable concept if you are alone and no longer have a use for it? Day and night; that's all you get.* Jon shook his head, conscious of the slap-slap of wavelets on the side of the boat. Obsessing about things that no longer served a purpose (or perhaps even existed!) saddened him. Was this sadness his way of processing loss? Or grief? He dipped an oar and followed the submerged rooftop edge until it rounded its underwater corner. Marking the power pole to his left he pushed on, noting the building corner and tracing an imaginary line along the water to where the next building should appear.

Thirty meters along his imaginary path a second spectral rooftop appeared, again another arm's length below the surface. The convenience store. Jon guessed an additional twenty meters would place him approximately in front of the entrance, so he pressed on for six more strokes. He shivered in anticipation of the dive. *What's the rush?* The young man stepped forward to the prow of the boat, grabbed the stone that was his makeshift anchor, and tossed it overboard. He watched the rope descend, and then tighten as it hit something, the sidewalk, he guessed, and then tied the slack to the rowlock to reduce drift.

In no rush — there was that time concept again — he sat back and listened to another Elliott Smith song, and thought about his good fortune at finding an abandoned, sort of operational solar panel farm, up in the hills. And he praised his good luck at finding it abandoned. There had been complications to his discovery, but all-in-all it became a fortunate decision to stay. The farm, together with the camp gave him a bit of warmth, light, music, and even enough power to cook things. Well, to warm things up, as thinning clouds permitted.

Jon scanned the horizon. It was an automatic gesture, signifying nothing. In the first days, when it rained day and night, he would spend a great part of the time in search of others. As the days grew in number and the instances of sightings reduced to zero — down from a total of two power boats disappearing south without so much as a wave — he stopped looking. Well, almost stopped. He had become aware of a pair of men — First Nations folk, he guessed — who would glide past from time to time, always lingering a half a kilometer away from the farm. Jon's effort at scanning the horizon produced the same as the others: a big fat nothing. Shrugging, he took off his boots and donned flippers. The net bag sat beside him, together with a flashlight and a hammer. His knife remained strapped to his calf, just in case.

A lungful of air lasted more than three minutes now, up from forty seconds. He noticed as the water warmed and after having found the wet suit, his energy wasn't dissipated through shivering, and he could extend his sorties underwater. The young man slipped over the side and wasted no time descending to the sidewalk. The store was (of course) dark and forbidding, and Jon was satisfied to see the plate glass windows all appeared intact. He tugged on the entrance from force of habit, and then hammered the window to the left. It shattered, and five more blows yielded a hole sufficient for entrance without risking a cut, always a dangerous possibility.

He kicked through the aperture that seconds earlier had been a window.

Jon thought with mild surprise how ordered the convenience store appeared, despite the passage of time since, well, since. He directed the ray of light in an arc across the width of the store.

The shelves that would normally carry potato chips sat bare. Most of the bags rested on the ceiling, many with expired dates, he supposed. Behind them, toward the back a solitary diapers box rested beside the non-functioning ceiling light. The others had reverted to pulp fibers and lay water-logged along the floor outside of the freezer doors. He swam toward the coolers, shining his flashlight behind the glass. A garish spectacle of purple, pink, and orange wisps of color threaded across the confined spaces behind the doors.

The spectral remains of Popsicles.

He moved on to the shelves lining the centre of the store. Canned goods, like obedient soldiers remaining on guard for thee. A moment later Jon cursed, remembering what would happen the moment he touched the cans. The paper labels would practically leap away from their tin partners, freed from the responsibility of proclaiming what food rested within each container. Mixing up the beans and the peaches appeared to be an inevitability, unless he made two trips. *Got any other plans for today? No? well then.* Jon began to gather up the cans of fruit, leaving the tinned meat and veg for the second trip. Before leaving the store, he gathered up a pair of coffee jars, a treat.

On his way back across the store, he tried not to imagine the fetid water contained within the convenience store. He took comfort in knowing he could keep his nose, mouth and eyes safely behind a face mask. The aperture reverted from entrance to exit, and the young man slipped out and then up the six meters to break the surface calm. He emptied the sack containing the tinned fruit, and again pulled himself down. The anchor line acted as both guide and impetus as he drew himself toward the spoils of his next trip: beans and other vegetables, stew, chili, and prepared meats.

But first, let's look for a treat, not yet spoiled. He began by swimming past the shelves and straight to the rear of the store. The door with the rusted sign 'Office' appeared interesting, and so he pried it open. The tiny area contained a desk, a filing cabinet, a wastepaper basket, and a corpse hanging, like meat curing in a freezer locker, from a ceiling light. With his light fixed on the body — not the face, Jon didn't care to look at the face — he saw little puffs of particulate, like smoke, seeping from the areas where cloth met skin. He backed out with as little movement as possible, and slowly closed the door as well as he could close a submerged, water-swollen, wooden door.

Jon's appetite for a treat had evaporated. He grabbed the tinned goods and propelled himself out of the once again darkened shop, and upward to charge his lungs, shudder, and slide into his boat.

The days had lengthened with the spring. Jon remembered as a child how much snow there had been to melt, and how his grandfather told of the spring storms that blew drifts high enough to walk right up onto the roofs of buildings. There were no worries about snow now, let alone snow drifts. And Jon remembered his mother fretting about the concept of climate change, and how people scoffed at her. 'But it's real!' she'd say. From his vantage point on Mactaquac Heights, Jon surveyed the water, a sea, really, that surrounded him. "Climate Change, indeed." Of course, once it had overwhelmed the world — what a difference two hundred feet of added sea levels made — most of the arses who professed willful ignorance had disappeared (together with most of those who had actually understood what had happened). Climate Change is an equal opportunity abuser, he thought.

"Another 'Warmest Spring Ever' headline for the day." Jon had taken to talking to himself since the last time he'd spoken with anyone. That last day, his neighbors had explained how sorry they were to have to leave him behind. 'Only so many seats,' they had said. 'You're the one of us who can survive alone for a while; we'll send a boat back as soon as we find a good chunk of land,' they had said. 'We love you!' They had said. The biggest lie of the three.

Once home, he performed a quick survey of the spit of land: any visitors, as evidenced by scuffing of the turf at the water's edge? No. Anything disturbed within or around the camp? No. He then proceeded to gather up a dozen portable lamps and freshly charged batteries from their resting place near the bank of batteries, and placed them on a small wooden ledge near the water. Chores done, he headed in to read a book.

That evening, he decided to leave the campfire to burn itself out. *I mean, where is it going to go?* But first he took a moment to study the vast skyscape of stars, and to listen to the quiet. He stood alone; so alone that even the birds, if there still were birds, failed to take wing across his tiny peninsula. His solar farm occupied half of the acreage of the tiny jut of land, and despite its size, only a fraction of the potential electricity of the panels came to fruition each day. More each day, but still nowhere near full capacity.

The sun rarely came out, and when it did show its face, it often peeked from behind wisps of fog; strands of moisture that argued the solar panels into a poverty of output. A month ago, the panels had barely worked. Then, they had relied upon as little as two or three hour's sunshine. It was better now. As a result, Jon completed activities requiring light following the start of the day. Once the sun set, he went to sleep. Or rather, he lay down with eyes closed until dawn, catching a half hour's sleep here and there over the course of the night.

One night during these in-between times he heard the scraping of a boat bottom at the water's edge nearby. Was it his neighbors from upriver? Thinking it couldn't be, his heartrate took a quick march up a steep hill. A discussion between Fight Jon and Flight Jon ceded the victory to 'I Don't Give A Shit Anymore' Jon. He waited, head cupped in one hand for his uninvited company to approach. The Statistics course from his past conjured up the probabilities of friendly folk seeking help versus armed intruders with no law or conscience to hold them back. The stats yielded a fifty-fifty chance of bad news outside his door. Jon's mind raced: *Did you ever want something as badly as you absolutely didn't want something?* Once the footsteps; tentative, he thought, *or maybe sneaky*, came to within three meters of his tiny camp, he called out. "The name is Jon. I'm unarmed. If you want to come in and kill me, make it quick."

There was no sound, at first, not even the quiet steps he'd heard seconds earlier. In a bit, a girl's voice, frail, called out. "I'm not here to hurt anyone. I just need a place to rest, and maybe eat something. I can trade stuff for food?"

Jon roused himself and opened the door to meet a young woman, possibly his age, standing part way between a Coleman canoe and his camp. She dropped a makeshift anchor onto the ground and stood, sizing him up. In turn, he took her measure, noting the arms hanging as if they weighed too much. He was certain that ninety per-cent of her energy was applied to remaining standing.

"When was the last time you ate?"

"Why?"

She offered zero trust, her stance all but saying she didn't want to fight, but would if need be. Jon suspected she couldn't remember when she had last eaten. He kept his tone flat, neutral. "Because if you are starved, I'll feed you, but if you're merely hungry, we can bring your stuff in to dry first. Or do you just want to get some sleep?"

"Dry clothes, then food, then sleep." Exhaustion washed the color from every word.

He left the steps and walked to the boat. The girl — even up close he couldn't gauge her age — pointed to a rucksack and a garbage bag, which he hauled out of the bowels of the canoe. She was soaked down one side, and he suspected she'd fallen while attempting to get the canoe partway up out of the water. She clutched a smaller backpack, stumbled on the top step and remained down on hands and knees. He hauled her up by one arm, she shuffled to the camp door, and together they entered the compact building.

The girl, who (now that he could see her in the light) he guessed to be twenty, eased over to the electric heater and plopped onto the floor directly in front of the grill. She muttered an obscenity. "I haven't seen electricity in action since ..." With the thought unfinished she raised a hand as if to make a point, but just let it drop and sat, eyeing him.

"Umm, you are asleep sitting up, but need food. I have nothing warm, so I could heat something or feed you cold beans." Her eyes had closed, so he shrugged and grabbed a half-eaten can of beans and a spoon from the counter. She ate the contents in three mouthfuls, put the can on the floor, as if it would take too much energy to lift it toward him, and struggled to swallow the last bit. He handed her a glass of water, which she emptied, and then she as much tipped over as settled into a spot on the floor. Jon fetched his pillow, lifted her head, and tucked the pillow under stringy, light brown hair. It being a warm evening, he placed a threadbare sheet over her, took off her sodden boots and socks and then spread her damp clothes across the kitchen table. He listened for the even breathing that would reveal she'd gone to sleep. Instead, he caught the wet rattle of a lung infection. After a bit, Jon switched off the lights. As was his habit, he opened his cell phone and spent the next few minutes searching for a signal. That done (*nothing, of course*), he lay down, faced the wall, and eventually drifted off to sleep.

Daylight beat her to consciousness by five hours. The woman had been coughing sporadically through the night, a wet rasp that impeded her breathing. A chest cold or something bacterial? *Bacterial or viral; a question of life or death?* Jon fretted about the response to that question. These days, certain events that had heretofore been dead easy to resolve had now become fraught with unexpected complexities. An eye infection, appendicitis, a broken leg; any of these could descend to something fatal. She coughed again, and this time rolled over.

Jon smiled as she faked being asleep while she got her bearings. "It's all good. You're safe." She opened one eye to study him, rolling up to a sitting position, with the sheet wrapped around her.

After a minute she spoke. "I'm Jamie. Thanks for this." She attempted a faint wave to encompass her surroundings, but because her hands were inside the sheet, Jon only saw the ghostly outline of fingers across cotton cloth. "Where are my socks? Umm, did you carry me in here?"

He shook his head, pointing to the table that held her entire wardrobe. "I brought in your clothes, but you half-walked, half-crawled in." He smiled. "Although I think it was a struggle. You seemed bone tired. The washroom is there," he pointed, "and I'll get you something to eat."

Jamie nodded and found her way to the bathroom, the threadbare sheet a cape. After a minute, she called out, "Are any of my clothes dry? I need a pair of pants; these got wet."

He gathered up the contents of the kitchen table in a single sweep and carried the lot over to the door. She took it all in and continued with her toiletries. He started opening cans for lunch. The coughing recommenced and Jon asked over his shoulder how she was feeling.

"Good. I have a cough. I can't see how it can be a cold, since I had no one to catch it from. It might be pneumonia, not the viral kind; the other kind, since my lungs hurt and I haven't been truly dry for more than a week."

"You taking anything for it?"

Silence. When she did speak, he could hear sarcasm dripping from her words. "The drug store doesn't seem to keep good business hours."

"Ah. A smart ass. You must be getting your energy back."

"Sorry. But there's no sense in wishing for drugs when there aren't any around. I expect staying dry for a while might help." More coughing.

"Do you have a fever?"

More silence. Then, "Possibly something low-grade. I'll be okay."

"Or not. After I feed you, I'm going out for a bit. Want to come with or stay here?"

"I am so tired. Can I sleep here for the day? I'll leave in the morning, if you want."

"Sure. No need to leave, though."

The late lunch consisted of a smoke-dried fish, coffee with canned milk, and a can of peaches. Jamie ate everything placed before her, and didn't ask for more, except for a top-up on the coffee. She did, however, make a point of staring at the salmon, over to his face, and then back to the fish. Jon made no effort at explaining how the salmon had come into his possession.

Once finished, he cleaned the dishes, made sure she noticed where he stored the can opener in the makeshift pantry. The young man, dressed in his wetsuit from the waist down, proceeded to gather foraging equipment together. "I'll be back in three or four hours. Help yourself to whatever you need." She had already slumped down before the heater, and had coughed twice before he had time to ease the camp door shut.

He rowed steadily for forty-five minutes, thinking about the stranger sleeping on the floor of the camp. His home. Why is she here? What does she want? How long will she stay? Would she steal anything, and did he even care? Jon had no answers by the time he arrived at the drug store on (above) Prospect Street. He employed the same routine: drop the anchor, descend to the store front, hammer in a window and swim through the opening to the pharmacy area. This time, the challenge was to find the drugs that hadn't been locked up in the large walk-in safe. Instead, Jon half-swam, half-walked to the shelves of prescriptions that had already been prepared and awaiting delivery. It took two trips back up for air before he could identify and grab the blister packs he sought, and make the lunge to the ceiling to where the plastic bottles of cough and pain pills remained floating, like so many miniature buoys. Satisfied, he bagged his prey and returned to the surface, picking up some bottled water and colas on the way.

Curious about something he noticed, Jon rowed past the convenience store on his return. Once there, he reached over the gunwale to touch the rooftop through the water. Satisfied with his discovery, he pushed away from the power pole and began his return to the camp.

Three-quarters of an hour later he arrived back home, noting the Coleman canoe sitting opposite last night's campfire. He walked in to Jamie sitting at the kitchen table, eating the remains of a can of tuna he had left in a tiny refrigerator created for college dorms. She tossed him a guilty look, but he smiled back. "All good. I told you to make yourself at home. Can we talk?"

She watched him take his wet clothes off and towel dry, turning to study the window at the appropriate moment of his undress. "Where did you go, if you don't mind me asking?"

"I went shopping at the pharmacy. Here." He withdrew a half dozen blister packs and analgesics from his webbed bag, tossing them on the table. "Some are a form of penicillin and the rest are not. The sun is out, which seldom happens. Let's go sit in the yard." Jon left the camp, rooting around for a shabby chair on his way out. "Sorry for the seating. I don't get company."

She sat beside the young man, facing the water and fidgeting with the blister packs of pills. He jumped back up and returned a moment later with a cola. "Might as well start in right away. They tend to bind you up, but our All Canned Goods diet will take care of that." They sat for a while, until Jamie broke the silence.

"Thank you. For this." She waved the pills. "And for the food. I didn't know what kind of reception I'd receive, but I only had enough strength to get to your campfire, so I had no choice but to see if you'd let me in. Is there any other, ah, people nearby?"

He shook his head in the negative. "You're pretty much the first one I've seen in a long time. Where did you come from?"

"Upriver. I live — lived — on a hillside. Most of my neighbors were swept away when the first dam broke, and the rest of them left by boat, I assume," her voice bitter, "one night. I was nursing my grandmother, and when I went to find food, I saw they had all gone. I hung out as long as I could, but little food, no heat, and no electricity left me no choice.

"I heard about a group when I was listening on my shortwave radio. When Nana died I got in the canoe and let it drift, heading toward the group. They're in Maine, I think. I notice the Beechwood Dam had also blown out, and I take it the Mactaquac Dam is gone too? It was just a big ol' concrete hole, when I drifted past." She coughed, making him wince.

Jon nodded. "Grand Falls is gone as well. They all went at the same time, as far as I can tell. What happened to your grandmother?"

"Yeah, no. She just went to sleep and didn't wake up. No medicine." She waved the blister pack, an encapsulation of her grief.

"So, have you thought about what you're going to do next?"

It was her turn to shake her head. "The plan is to head to Maine, but exactly when depends on what you have to say. Can I hang out here for a day or two?" A half-smile formed. "Or three?" He thought she looked younger when she smiled.

He returned her smile. "Sure. We'll talk about this again in three days. You may be sick of me by then, and I promise you that infection won't have cleared up in only forty-eight hours. I don't know what has been on your mind up 'til now." He knew very well that survival was all she thought of, because that was all there was left. "But all there is to do for the next while is eat if you're hungry or sleep if you're sleepy. I'll take care of the rest for now."

He changed gears. "Are you kind? Are you a kind person?"

Jamie smiled without humor. "Is this a first date? Are we on some kind of dating show?"

Jon shrugged. "A cynic might say how you answer that question could determine how long you get to stay. But really, I was just trying to make small talk." They sat beside each other, staring through the awkwardness until Jon changed the subject again. "Hey, do you want to hear some news?"

"Where on earth did you get news from? Did you pick up something from the airwaves? A radio signal? I have a shortwave radio, by the way, but no batteries anymore."

"No. Remember me telling you I visited a convenience store yesterday? Well, a week ago I couldn't touch the roof from my boat. With my arm. Today I could stand on it without getting my ankles wet. The water has gone down at least a couple of feet."

She shook her head, disbelieving. "That makes no sense. Climate change doesn't reverse."

"Maybe not, but if three dams blow out during climate change, the water from upriver would have nowhere to go, especially during the spring freshet. It can take weeks — a month! — to dissipate. I don't think I'm wrong; the water is receding. This doesn't help Saint John, but we may begin to see more land around here soon. I hope so."

"Maybe." She didn't look convinced. "I have to go lie down."

"Take my bed. I'm going to sun myself for a bit. Get some Vitamin D." He watched her retreating figure, unexpectedly pleased with the presence of another human, even a grumpy one. He studied the horizon, noticing the two men from upriver who had again stopped by to watch. A crow landed on a nearby fir, and it took Jon ten minutes to realize this was the first animal he'd seen in more than a month.

The young woman took three days and more to convalesce. The fever disappeared in forty-eight hours, and the bouts of coughing slowed shortly thereafter. Jamie's energy was the last symptom to return to normal, and she volunteered to help him go 'grocery shopping' after the third day. Jon noticed the camp became tidier, and certain chores including collecting driftwood magically happened when he wasn't around.

One evening as they sat reading, Jamie scratched at the top of the table with a fingernail, staring at the scarred wood, and again asked him what he saw for himself in the future.

"I honestly don't know yet. I've been watching the Prospect Street rooftops, and most of them are now peeking out above the water. And it's only been three days. The water is receding, and I'd like to get a sense of how far down it will go before it stops. Are you getting itchy to leave?" He couldn't tell if her look of pique was for the honesty of the question, or toward him directly, so he waited.

"I mean, we can't stay here forever, can we? The food will run out sooner or later. I think it's a matter of when we go, and not if, right?"

Jon's voice was patient. "It's tricky. I'm waiting for a certain something to happen, which will force my hand. In the meantime, if the water continues to go down, and if the food holds up, we can stay a while longer. And if we leave too early and someone comes along, this place becomes ... contentious, and we're back to possessing the boats we have, and that's it."

"If, if, if. I know how lucky I was to find this place. To find you.

You have been ... well, a life saver. In normal times, I'd have loved to have met you in a bar, or in the mall, you know; someplace normal, and we could have been a couple of kids having fun. Instead, well I don't know about you, but with all the company we've been having," that sarcasm again, "we have to seriously consider whether we're the last ones to survive." She blushed at the implications of her words. He shook his head, but didn't challenge her opinion.

She raised both hands, impatient. "Here we have lots of canned goods, but soon they'll be rusty when we get to them. If the water goes down, we could plant, and maybe even fish, but what would we plant with? All the seeds must be rotten by now, so where does that leave us?"

Her voice grew quieter. "But the other thing is, I'm not brave. I'm not sure if I'm brave enough to leave here alone. Without you. I'm pretty sure I wouldn't have lasted another day if I hadn't met ... if you weren't ... I know it's only been a few days, and a cynical person may say I want you as a second body, my so-called strong man protector." She returned her hands onto the table top, her voice just above a whisper. "But I'm getting to know you, and if I have to walk whatever spots remain on this earth, I'd rather you were by my side. Besides, if you stayed behind, I'd worry about you. Because if the water is up or the water is down, things will get worse, before they get even worse."

They sat in silence, pondering each others' words. Jon crossed the room and picked up her shortwave radio. He looked self-conscious. "I've been playing with this since I recharged it yesterday. I, um, found some people, probably the ones you were talking about, you know; the ones you heard when you were upriver. I don't know where they are, actually, but they did mention our region. Most of coastal Nova Scotia is gone, and all of Prince Edward Island, so I expect they are somewhere in New Brunswick or Maine. Probably Maine." He paused, waiting for her reaction.

"When were you going to tell me?"

"Apparently, one day after I heard them. The voices, I mean. Look; your radio wasn't even working yesterday afternoon, I came across them last evening, and now it's noon. Clearly I haven't been sitting on this."

"I'm sorry. It's just ... this is big news. We're not alone." It was her turn to pause. "So, does this change your mind, you know, about going?"

"I was thinking, if we listened to them, just for a bit, we could figure out where they are, what their circumstances are, and if, you know ... if they're kind." He added, "One guy kept asking if anyone is out there, and he gave his Latitude and Longitude coordinates. So maybe they're open to taking people in. I don't know, it's all so uncertain..."

"So, you want to creep them for a bit. Just listen and see what their deal is. That can't hurt, right?"

Jon thought of the saying 'Be careful what you ask for; you just might get it.' Aloud he said, "I suppose."

Jamie gave him a smile and a hug. "You didn't know what you were getting when you took me in, right?" An extra little squeeze and she released him.

"Truer words ..." He left the remainder of the axiom hanging.

That evening they listened to the shortwave broadcast Jon had found. Indeed, some of the people speaking had Maine accents, and Jamie touched Jon's arm every time mention was made of food. It seemed the group had been able to save bags of seeds in a giant barn on a hill, and the waters in that area had also begun to drop. By the end of the broadcast, Jamie had shifted to sit beside him, one hand on his shoulder.

They sat back, as if they'd been watching some sort of epic concert. "So, what d'ya think?"

Jon studied her, noting the brightness in her eyes, the elevated breathing, and the fact she hadn't coughed the entire time they had listened to the broadcast. "I'm running out of reasons to stay. Except ..."

The corners of her mouth turned down, assuming a more neutral expression. "Except?" She paused. "Because, I've literally run out of reasons." She withdrew her arm in a quiet movement, and threaded her fingers together into a prayer-like sculpture.

"You heard that old guy say he wasn't sure how things will be around there in the upcoming year."

Jamie tried to put a positive spin on it. "Oh, you know old people; they used up all their optimism years ago. And the rest of them seemed to want more people, and by that I bet they mean younger people to come help. Do you want to take some time; maybe think about what you've heard?"

He knew it was what she wanted, so he nodded. It rained again that night, a cold rain.

The next morning, just after dawn, Jon stood over Jamie, shaking her shoulder. "Wake up. We have company. She sat bolt upright, grabbing for her jeans near the foot of the bed. "Stall them for twenty seconds."

"No need. They're a ways off yet."

Jon and Jamie moved to the water's edge and watched and waited as a rowboat drew closer, tugging a tender that appeared to be a modified raft. Two men in the lead boat pulled on a pair of oars, the tether boat swishing from side to side, just a bit, as it followed.

Jamie whispered, her lips barely moving. "I don't know them. Do you?"

"Uh huh. These are the people who left me behind."

"Oh, shit! What does it mean?"

"We're about to find out, I suppose."

The man on the right stopped rowing, turning around to greet the couple on the shore as they drifted closer.

"Jonny! Long time, no see." The boat nudged the shoreline and the man who had first stopped rowing jumped from the boat and strode toward them. He offered up a broad smile, with his eyebrows canted in a look of apology and a right hand outstretched. "It has been a while, sorry about that. It took us some time to get situated, but here we are, back for you as promised."

"Back for you?" Jamie mouthed the words as much as said them.

Jon felt fingers dig into his arm. The second man disembarked and the pair introduced themselves as Henry and Pernell.

The young couple brought the men into the camp, asking if they were hungry or thirsty. "How about some coffee and then we can chat."

As he gathered the ingredients for coffee, Jon noticed Jamie hadn't said a word, although both men made small talk, oblivious to the tension. Coffee sorted, they sat down to face one another. Jon began.

"So, did you find a place to land? I guess so, or you would have been back sooner."

Henry nodded. "Indeed. We let the river take us down toward Saint John, but really, there was nothing left of the city. So we went north and east …"

"To Moncton."

Henry nodded. "Yes. Moncton was basically gone, but the surrounding hillside: Lutes Mountain and Magnetic Hill survived the flooding. We found a small community, well, fifteen people and a barn, and we set up homesteading. It's snug —" he cast a sideways glance toward Jamie "— but we're making a go of it."

Jon nodded, watching Jamie watching him. "Tight, eh?" He paused, studying the floor. "How tight?"

Pernell spoke up. "Pretty tight. We could take, ah, one more." He gestured outside, to the already laden rowboat.

"And what do you need? I expect there is a — the colony is probably short of something?"

The men cast a self-conscious look at each other. "Since you brought it up, we recalled you sitting on a significant solar farm next door. We have an operating wind farm, but don't have the technology or tools to maintain it. Once it's gone, well, we have to look elsewhere for electrical sources. The farm here could easily run if it was missing a few panels and a few batteries …" Neither one looked anywhere in the direction of the woman.

Jamie spoke at last, without making eye contact with anyone in the tiny room. "This is actually good news. Jon and I were chatting last night about this. I'm heading off tomorrow to Maine. A community over there invited me to come by." Her tone dry, she continued. "It seems that they have the very same price of admission."

Henry jumped in. "Look, we'd take you both in a heartbeat if there was room. But there just isn't. Our land can only sustain so many ... bodies." He focussed his attention on Jon. "Katrina was asking about you. She's hoping you are healthy and interested in coming back with us."

Jon reached over to take Jamie's hand. She pulled it away as if it had been scalded. An uncomfortable silence flooded the room.

Pernell stood up. "I expect you two have a few things to, ah, talk about. Henry and I will go stretch our legs, maybe look over the three solar panels we're taking." They each took a mug and left the camp, with Jamie and Jon staring at the floor.

After an eternity, Jon looked over to Jamie, and again tried to take her hand. This third effort was refused, but Jon insisted, holding her fingers as he moved closer. "Let's go outside. I want to show you something. Two things, actually." They left the cabin and he tugged a less-than-willing Jamie down to the water's edge. On the way, he pointed to a rock he had placed a week earlier. "This is where the water was when you got here." They continued another ten yards until their toes met the water's edge. "And this is where it is now. In one week. But that's not what I brought you here to see." He pointed north, a quarter of a mile away.

"That's a canoe! What the hell?"

Jon waved in an exaggerated gesture, and the figures in the canoe began moving toward the young couple. "It's some men I met, from Kingsclear. They kind of watch over me. In turn, I watch over their solar farm."

Jamie switched her gaze from the paddlers back to Jon, staring without saying anything.

"I know, I know. When was I going to say anything? Here's the thing." He jammed his hands deep into his jeans pockets. "I didn't say anything at first because I don't tell strangers what I'm thinking; I just don't. And even after I got to know you, I didn't say anything because I promised them." He jerked a thumb out toward the water and the approaching canoe. I also thought, what if you wanted — I mean, *really* wanted — to do something with this information and I didn't want ... the same thing? So I held off, thinking I could tell you when we needed this information to make a decision. And I guess the time is now." The canoers had almost reached shore, catching the attention of the first arrivals of the day.

On his way to the waterline, Pernell called out. "What's this, then? What's going on?"

Jamie's head swiveled from the strangers on land to the strangers in the boat. Her eyes stopped once they came to rest on Jon, and her eyebrows fixed in a quizzical pose.

The canoe glided to the shoreline, and both arrivals sat still, paddles resting across the gunwales in front of each. "*Qey.*" One spoke. Everyone looked to Jon.

Jon moved to the water's edge, taking the line they offered. "*Qey,* Edwin, hello Albert. Your lanterns and batteries are all charged and ready for you to take back to Kingsclear. In the meantime, these men would like to take three solar panels and some batteries from your solar farm." He emphasized the number three, as well as the word 'your'.

Henry smiled, an act that didn't quite reach his eyes. "It's *their* farm. I guess we asked the wrong person for the gift of solar panels."

Jon leaned in toward Jamie, and asked her to accompany him to the cabin. Upon her nod, he looked to both small groups. "Jamie and I have something to say to each other. We'll just be a minute." They returned to the cabin and he turned to face her. "Here are your options: you set out alone for Maine, you return with these two men to Lutes Mountain without me, or you agree to follow these new friends of mine to Kingsclear, half an hour away."

She gave him a look he couldn't read. "Pros and cons?"

"I don't like the men from Lutes Mountain. They left me behind once, and they are prepared to divide us up. Not to mention they are trying to bully us into giving them more than my neighbors can afford to give. To their credit, they did come back, but I don't really think it was for me." He continued.

"We agreed that staying here isn't really an option. So, no pro there.

"Going to Maine is a possibility, but you're buying a pig in a bag; who knows how that will turn out? The kicker for me is you'd have to go alone, since I'm not going.

"And Kingsclear? I trust these people. And their setup is good. They're mostly First Nations people, and they know all about native pharmaceuticals. And they didn't ask me for anything except to let them know when I wanted to join them. They appointed me The Watcher here. I watch the farm, and they've been watching over me. And they'd be happy to take both of us in. And yes; that's where the salmon came from."

Jamie studied him, her face uncertain. "And what about us?"

"I'd love for there to be an 'us'. We can have that at Kingsclear, if you want. I think you know by now that I'm no risk-taker, which is why I don't want Lutes Mountain or Maine. And I can't stay here anymore, since Edwin and Albert and the other First Nations people are going to bring the solar farm to Kingsclear, mostly because of the Henrys and Pernells of the world. Besides, you've already talked me out of staying here any longer. So ... you now know where I stand. Beside you, if I can." He waited, uncertainty written all over him.

Jamie withdrew a compact blister pack from her jeans pocket. He noticed it was an unopened container of the antibiotics she'd received from his sortie a week earlier. She touched every part of it, as if the package was more talisman than medicine. Her voice when she began to speak conveyed thoughts that welled up from deep within her. "I don't remember much about the day you went out and got these. That was Day Two for us and I was *so* sick, although I tried not to show it. I keep these in my pocket even though I'm done with them, but every time I touch the packet, I think of you, and how you didn't have to do that for a stranger.

"Kindness is a big deal for me, and it was the first thing that drew me to you. Whatever happens next, let's do it together."

The couple returned to the shoreline, to where the four others were in conversation. Henry faced Jon, who noted that the man now stood directly between Jon and the pair in the canoe. Was it deliberate?

Henry traced a circle in the dirt with a stick he'd found. "So, what's it to be? Are you coming with us, Jonnie?"

Jon leaned sideways, so that his shoulder now touched Jamie's. "We love it here, and have decided that we will stay in the area, dividing our time between Kingsclear and my home here. I'll remain the guardian of the solar farm until they move it closer, and we'll grow things in Kingsclear, once the water settles a bit. Thank you for the kind offer, and we'll help you gather up one solar panel and the batteries and gear needed to run it."

"Just the one panel?" Pernell's eyes had narrowed, his jaw set.

The man in the canoe who had remained seated in the rear spoke up. "The land this farm is sitting on belongs to my community. We would be pleased to help you load one panel, but our community of forty needs the others." They rose and stood alongside their canoe.

Pernell's face took on a stubborn demeanor. "Now, that doesn't feel very generous."

The man stood stoic, with no expression that could be read. "If a guest visits a farmer, they can expect a meal. Seldom are they invited to load their vehicle with as much of the crop as they can carry away. One solar panel is generous, and we will help you load it." The transfer of the panel and accompanying gear took twenty minutes as Jamie and Jon made the men a modest lunch. Henry and Pernell left with neither a word nor a backward glance.

Edwin stared at the retreating boats. "Another reason to move the solar farm a bit closer."

Chuck Bowie

Chuck studied Science at the University of New Brunswick, in Canada. His writing is influenced by the study of Human Nature and how people behave. He loves food, wine, music, and travel, and all play a role in his work. His latest novel is entitled *Her Irish Boyfriend*, fifth in the international thriller series **Donovan: Thief 4 Hire**. He has just completed the third novel in a new cozy mystery series: **Old Manse Mysteries**, set in a small Atlantic Canadian town.

Chuck has sat on the Boards of The Writers' Union of Canada and the Writers' Federation of New Brunswick. He is a Fellow of the Kingsbrae International Residency for the Arts, and is an author of note with the Miramichi Literary Trail.

www.chuckbowie.ca

Erasing

By S. C. Eston

I STOOD TRANSFIXED AS FLOATING SILHOUETTES emerged above the western horizon. One by one, the figures glided into view, moving swiftly above the rolling fields and the patches of star-shaped red blooms, unfazed by the flowers' proud announcement that springtime was upon us. The early morning sun cast long shadows that struggled to keep up with the gliding invaders.

"They will come," mother had warned more than a year ago.

I had never seen a Sentinel before. Never dreamed I would. Never wanted to.

Now, sixteen had come.

The bag I was holding slipped out of my numb fingers and disappeared into the grass at my feet. Ahead, the silhouettes converged at the highest elevation of the western hills. There they closed ranks and consulted with each other. One pointed north. Another, the tallest, turned my way.

I dropped down like a falling tree. The air burst out of my lungs on contact with the ground, but I abstained from crying. The long grass was strewn with the mushrooms I had painstakingly gathered.

"You got that, Sirka?" mother had asked before I left that morning. "Only pick those that are at least one-third purple. Leave the others for later. Two dozen should do it."

The fungi were the main ingredient of a hot brew mother prepared every night for sister. It kept nightmares away, and without it, she couldn't sleep.

Thinking of sister brought me back to the danger now roaming our land. I had to get home and warn mother and father.

Staying low, I grabbed as many of the pink and purple mushrooms as I could and placed them back in the bag. Then, carefully pushing aside a clump of green grass, I looked west.

The Sentinels were now heading north, toward the never-ending white wall barely visible beyond the high mounds. Close behind them, an unkindness of ravens appeared, tarnishing the flawless cerulean sky. The birds' arrival was followed by the unmistakable howling of wolves.

Ravens and wolves.

Following their masters.

My hands trembled uncontrollably. Bringing them together didn't help.

"They will come," mother had warned. "One day they will return and they will find us."

I didn't head back to the village at once. Instead, I rushed south until I reached the Secret Grove. At least that's what sister and I called the serene little clearing hidden along the northern bank of the river.

"Sister!" I announced as I forced my way through a thick shrub of golden forsythia.

A loud shushing sound and a raised finger welcomed me as I stepped into the glade. Sister knelt in the grass, a ruby robin in the open palm of her other hand, its bright scarlet chest matching her disheveled hair.

Any other day, I would have stood back and admired the scene, enjoying the rare peace sister found in this place. I often wondered if my baby sister knew that she was my world. I would have given anything to have her smile again, have her talk again, have her sleep a dreamless sleep again.

Today, though, I slowly made my way to her side, knelt, and whispered: "We have to go."

She shook her head with impatience, sending her fiery hair into a frenzy. With a sharp gesture of her raised finger, she asked for a moment longer. The hatchling on her hand retreated into a red and black ball of feathers, as if sensing danger.

"Now," I said, taking hold of her shoulder.

Sister looked at me, anger brewing in her eyes, and blurted out incoherent words that I managed to decipher as meaning that she knew. I should have realized that she would have sensed the Sentinels' presence already, probably long before they appeared on the horizon before me.

Four years ago, something had changed her. She had been two then and the consternation and hopelessness on my parents' face still haunted me. They hadn't known what had happened, how it had happened, or why. Suddenly, sister started to feel the world around us, its life force, its mood, sometimes its pain. It changed her, took away her happiness, her ability to speak, to smile.

I studied her, wondering why she hadn't already run back to the village. Her hair floated around her face and the energy it exuded was almost tangible. Did she know something I didn't?

"You can feel them, right?"

She nodded, her anger transforming into angst as she looked at me. Although she said nothing, I knew that somehow she had been waiting for me. She lifted her finger again.

"Just a moment," I said. "Be quick."

Turning away, she crawled forward, keeping her palm up, all the way to the nest concealed under the low branches of a second golden shrub. There, she delicately placed the baby bird down, patting it gently, fondly.

I savored the moment, taking in the muted burble of the river as its water jumped over rocks, smiling as the robin made a sweet and mumbled cooing sound. I quietly thanked sister because I had a premonition that we would never return to this glade again.

Our passage through the village was a blur, leaving chaos and panic behind as I yelled that *they* were here. No one asked who *they* were. Everybody knew about mother's warning and had been afraid of the day the Sentinels would arrive. That fear had been exacerbated about a month ago, when we found a strange disk in the ground on the other side of the white wall.

Sister's hand felt small in mine as we approached the village's council hall. I squeezed, letting her know that I was here.

My little sister had discovered the disk. It had first called to her in the middle of the night and her anguished cries had woken me up. I jumped out of my cot and dove to her side, my heart trying to leap out of my chest. Mother and father burst in the room an instant later. Sister wasn't aware of our presence, didn't hear our words. She held both hands extended in front of her, as if reaching for something.

The next day, the three of us followed her. The councillors and many others from the village joined our march. Sister led us to a place where the white wall disappeared under a high plateau. Climbing up the elevated plain allowed us to cross over the wall without touching it. We followed her far to the north, in the forbidden domains hanging between this world and oblivion. She finally stopped and collapsed in front of a strange disk in the ground.

Mother and father's hopes had been that the disk would somehow free sister, bringing back the happy little girl we missed so deeply.

It hadn't.

And now...the Sentinels were here.

I looked up and over the roof of the council hall and caught a glimpse of the Red Lady's statue. It stood on top of the cliff, to the right of the gushing waterfalls. If ever there was a time to pray to Shillis, this was it.

"Keep us warm," I whispered. "Keep us safe."

Using two hands, I pushed open one of the large double doors. As soon as we stepped inside the hall, it creaked back into place. We made our way along columns and under arches. My gaze kept going to the sculptures decorating the wood, scenes created by the Carvers of

Shalyrium and offered as a present to the founder of our village more than a hundred and sixty years ago. Before founding our village, Armana had been a member of the Carvers herself. After retiring, she left Shalyr and made her way around the Desolation all the way to this gorge. Her modest abode still stood at the foot of the waterfall, transformed into a shrine. Our family visited it from time to time to meditate.

Sister and I reached the steps leading up to the assembly chamber. As we climbed, the five councillors appeared, seated in their high chairs, lost in discussion. Although the seats formed a half circle facing us, they didn't notice our arrival.

"We're leaving tomorrow morning," said father, his voice booming through the hall. "This is an opportunity we can't miss."

I stole a glance to my right, where an imposing door loomed at the end of a dark corridor. Behind it...

"I doubt the wisdom in rushing back north," said Celista, the eldest of the councillors. She sat in the middle, mother on her right, father on her left. Aldel, Celista's own younger sister, sat to the far right. Faria, the tallest of the councillors, listened from the far left.

"We need to study it to understand it," said father. "Twelve have already volunteered to accompany me."

Faria shook her head. "You should have consulted with us prior to forming a company."

"I asked to meet, remember?"

Faria looked away, Aldel down at her feet. Only mother and Celista didn't flinch.

"I remember," said Celista. "We had every intention of answering your request."

"But you haven't," father said.

"What do you think?" Celista asked of mother.

I knew that my parents didn't agree on what to do with the disk. Mother's interest in it had been solely in the hope that it could help sister. Father, on the other hand, seemed to have developed an unhealthy obsession with the object.

"I agree that there might be value in studying it," mother said, "but I'm also wary of traversing the Palisade." That's how mother referred to the white wall.

"I share Saria's concerns," said Aldel. "We already sent three expeditions and learned little. With each crossing, the chances of drawing unwanted attention grow."

"But don't you see what we have?" asked father. "Don't you..." He noticed sister and me and fell silent.

Mother followed his gaze and saw us. "Sirka, what are you doing here?"

The other three councillors slowly turned our way. I felt sister slide behind me.

"It's too late," I said.

"What do you mean, child?" asked Celista.

"It's too late, madam. They are already here."

The colors withdrew from the councillors' faces. I reached back and clasped one of sister's hands in mine, squeezing it. She squeezed back.

Celista stared down at us, as if lost. After a moment, she finally spoke: "Sirka, what are you saying?"

I thought my words had been quite clear. I looked at mother, but her attention was on sister, who now stood by my side, lower lip trembling, fiery hair dancing around her face.

"You can feel them, can't you?" mother asked.

A strange coldness emanated from sister's body. Her whole frame shook. I brought one of her hands in front of me and held it there. She looked at me, then at mother, and nodded once.

"How many?" asked Celista. "How many did you see?"

Her voice betrayed the control and calmness she was trying to portray.

"Sixteen, madam," I said. "I counted sixteen."

For a moment, it looked as if Celista was going to faint. Aldel swiftly joined her older sister, holding her up.

Mother took this opportunity to cross the space between us and enveloped sister in her arms. Father promptly appeared beside her.

"Are you certain?" he asked, putting a hand on sister's shoulder.

"Yes," I said. "I was collecting these when I saw them."

I lifted the bag of mushrooms as if it proved my words. The sack looked out of place and suddenly quite superfluous. I dropped it to the floor. The rolling pink and purple fungi clashed against the washed-out floorboards.

"We should not have crossed the wall," said Faria, still in her seat. "We should have known better," she added.

Father didn't let go of sister's shoulder. "There was no way to know," he said. "They tell us nothing and we had an opportunity, a chance to learn about where we live, about our world. We had to take it. It was the right thing to do. The only thing to do."

"But why are they here now?" insisted Faria. "Why not two weeks ago, when—"

"Not in front of the children," interrupted Celista.

Mother nodded at the elder and then proceeded to escort us down the steps and all the way out of the hall.

"It's unlocked," I said, out of breath.

We had just run around the council hall, all the way to its alternate door located on the river side. Rarely used, it hid under a wooden arch covered in pink wisteria. The pea-like clusters reminded me of the pinkish shade of the mushrooms I had collected earlier.

Sister's hair was disheveled, and a redness appeared in her cheeks. Always the impatient, she indicated the door with a movement of her head.

I hesitated, uncertain if I wanted to disobey mother.

Sister mumbled a few words, some clearer than usual. She wanted to know what the councillors were going to decide. She poked me in the chest with her index finger, emphasizing that I was the one who had brought them the news of the Sentinels' arrival.

"I know," I said, the obvious somehow making me indignant. "Follow me."

The door opened with a creak and we edged inside. I led the way, and after crossing a small vestibule and a short corridor, we came to the main room. We passed in front of the councillors' empty seats and went directly to the hallway shrouded in shadows, all the way to its door. We both pushed against it and, to our relief, it slid open without a sound.

Leaving the door ajar, we slipped inside. I had bad memories of the place because of how severely we had been chastised the last time we snuck in. Like I remembered from the brief glimpse I caught then, heavy red drapes fell from the ceiling, encapsulating the center of the room, hiding those within from us. Hiding the room's dark secret, which we had failed to witness at that time.

Walking on tiptoes, we made our way around the periphery until we reached a slight opening in the curtains.

We peeked inside.

Three steps led down to a recessed floor. There, four columns formed a square and held the white dome above. The councillors stood close together, their backs to us. Mother moved and I gasped.

In the center of the space, the impossible presented itself to us.

A Sentinel.

Inert, lying on a large stone slab.

His cape cascaded down the side of the table. His eyes were closed, his hands resting flat at his sides, the symbols tattooed on his forearms barely visible. One could easily have assumed him to be in a restful sleep, if not for the dagger lodged in the middle of his torso.

"It can't be him," I heard Celista say. "He hasn't moved. The dagger hasn't moved."

Even so, the sight of the Sentinel on his back, so close, made me fearful. Sister nuzzled against my side and I put an arm around her. She was trembling. I wanted to tell her that everything would be all right, but I couldn't.

"We don't know," mother said. "It could be the disk, the fact that we crossed the Palisade, or this Sentinel, missing."

"It was bound to happen," said Aldel. "We've been playing with fire."

"But why now?" asked father. "They've ignored us for so long."

I noticed that the Sentinel's chest was moving up and down, ever so faintly, lifting the dagger with it. He was alive. What kind of weapon could neutralize a Sentinel this way?

"It's the sum of it all," proposed Celista. "Our time is done."

"We just don't know," repeated mother. "Let's not speculate. They are here, today. That's where our energy should go."

"Well said," said Celista. "Let's notify the village. It is time to retreat—"

A loud clap shook the building and swallowed the elder's voice. The world shifted around us. The floor dropped slightly and I fell to my knees. Sister stood, but only because her fingers grasped my shoulder.

"What was that?" I whispered, barely able to push the words out. The air felt empty. I took several long breaths but ended up fatigued.

"Did you all feel that?" echoed father from the other side of the curtains. His voice also came with difficulty.

Before anyone could answer him, a second powerful and distant crack resounded. A swooshing sound followed immediately, reminding me of the wind during a storm. The resonance didn't stop. Instead, it amplified itself, becoming louder, as if it was fast approaching, turning into a shriek...of rage, of pain.

Taken by fear, I lay down and pulled sister with me. She huddled against my chest and I wrapped my arms around her small body. Under the curtains, I found mother prone on the floor, staring directly at me, my distress reflected in her eyes. She said something, but her voice couldn't pierce the din.

As suddenly as it had come, the commotion stopped, ending in a slurping sound, as if something had siphoned it away.

I opened my eyes, unable to remember when I had closed them. "Are you all right?"

Sister shook her head, her eyes tearing up. I moved back, keeping her at arm's length, and examined her. She seemed uninjured, but her skin felt like ice. I couldn't stop panic from taking hold of me.

"Mother!" I yelled. "MOTHER!"

The curtains opened and mother appeared. Behind her, the councillors were getting back on their feet, each one obviously shaken by what had happened. I noticed father caring for Celista.

"Look at me," mother told sister. "My sweet little girl, look at me."

Sister did and seemed to calm down, although her hair didn't settle. It danced in front of her eyes as if taken by lunacy, its bright scarlet tint gone. Instead, it was a dark russet, as if dried out.

Mother gave her an extended embrace, rubbing her back as she did so. "Everything will be all right," she said.

I still held on to one of sister's hands, while feeling like something was not quite right. It felt like we were alone in the world. No, it felt as if the rest of the world had gone away somehow.

Mother let go and looked at me. "Sirka, whatever you do, don't let go of her. Do you understand me?"

"Yes."

"Ralka," mother called. "We have to go. Now."

Father joined us. He kissed sister on the head and hugged me briefly with one arm. "Let's go," he said.

Together, we left the other councillors and the Sentinel behind, made our way through the main room and out the front door. As soon as we stepped into the cool spring air, the feeling of wrongness assailed me again, except this time it was much more dominant. Father halted, bringing us all to a stop.

"What is happening?" he said.

Mother didn't answer. Instead, she looked up toward the sky. "You see it, don't you?"

I glanced at sister and saw that her lower lip was trembling. The cold touch of her fingers in mine was beginning to be painful. I followed mother's gaze but couldn't see anything special. At least not at first. Then elongated wisps appeared, partly transparent, distorting the infinite blue of the sky, slithering from north to south.

"What are those?" I asked.

"Saria, what do you think is happening?" father asked again. Using mother's name got her attention.

She shook her head slowly, as if in disbelief. "You know what this is."

Father stared at her, his eyes wide. "I thought...I thought those were only stories."

"We knew it was possible," she said. "We just decided to turn a blind eye."

"They can't be doing this," father said.

Mother put an arm around father and he returned the gesture. They hugged and somehow looked so small.

"They are," said mother. "Shillis save us all."

Screams rose from somewhere in the village, making sister and me jump. Father and mother brought us closer, mother holding on to sister, father to me.

"Should we go to the house?" asked father.

"I don't think so," mother said in a voice I didn't recognize. "I think we should leave now."

"What's happening?" I asked.

Instead of answering, our parents looked around, down the road, to the other side of the river. People were in disarray, some running, some seemingly lost, many staring at the sky.

The air still tasted empty. Even after inhaling two or three times, I felt like it wasn't enough. The swooshing sound from earlier had returned, but as a continuous hum barely audible in the distance.

"Let's leave now, Ralka," mother said to father. Her arms tightened around sister. "We'll figure things out after we're away."

Father looked at me. "Where did you see them?"

I pointed to the northwest.

"We'll go east then." He took hold of my hand and guided us down the road, toward the bridge. Roofs in the northern part of the village appeared to float between branches, some covered in buds, others in full bloom, a few enveloped in greenery. Along the western road, people had amassed, some with bags hanging from their shoulders or backs. We were not the only ones hoping to escape the village. Ahead of the main throng, a man was gesticulating in front of a horse pulling a cart. A young boy and girl, with an older woman, sat in the cart. From this distance, I couldn't make out who these people were.

"Why have they stopped?" I asked, thinking that if the intent was to flee, they needed to turn around and go east.

"I think it's too late," father said, stopping suddenly. He looked back the way we came, then to the east again.

"Too late for what?" I asked.

It was mother who answered. "To leave, my dear. It's too late to leave."

Dread trickled down my spine.

A new series of screams reached our ears. I returned my gaze to the western road, and there the wisps had taken a material form and now extended toward the man and his cart. Lightning bolts of energy flashed up and down in front of him, along what looked like a barrier of mist. Suddenly, a tendril lashed out and took hold of the man's leg. It tripped him and dragged him down the road. Another white tentacle followed, grabbing the horse around the neck. The animal reared, fighting against the tendril's hold. It stepped sideways and the cart started to topple.

Then several additional wisps appeared and surrounded the cart and grabbed its passengers.

"What is that cart doing there?" I asked.

Along the western road, a lone cart rested on its side. It had obviously been pulled there, but by whom, or when, it was impossible to say. I stared at it and felt that something was missing. Even more peculiar, I had the feeling that I knew what was missing but couldn't quite remember.

"It has begun," father said.

"I know," mother replied.

"I can't believe what is happening, can't believe it's true. Even less that it's happening to us."

A single tear escaped from one of mother's eyes and rolled down her cheek.

"Mother, what is going on?" My words were barely audible, a low murmur, and yet mother turned my way.

She put a hand on the side of my face, squeezed my cheek fondly. "Erased," she said. "We're being erased."

My head spun. My lungs cried for air. I looked down at sister, who was trembling with fear against mother's chest. I bent down and kissed her on the head, worried about the paleness and coldness of her skin.

"It's moving," father said. "Getting closer. We have to move."

And yet he didn't and continued to gape toward the west. There, on the road, two people fell to their knees, grabbed each other, hugged, became one, before they were suddenly taken from the dirt and tugged away by two long intertwining tentacles. Behind them, a large golden bush swayed to the left, its branches stretched and twisted, its flowers torn and sucked away...the whole bush was uprooted and nothing remained.

Nothing except an uncanny blank canvas.

Had someone been there, on the empty road?

"It's going to swallow the whole village," mother said.

I looked up and noticed that the pulsating haze hung in the sky as well, blocking the sun.

"Who's doing this?" I asked.

"The Sentinels, my dear," mother said.

"What...what can we do?"

"Stay together."

"Let's head back toward the hall," father said. I had never seen him like this. His shoulders sloped down and the spark in his eyes, the one that had blazed to new heights recently when the disk was found, was almost completely gone. "Let's keep away from that thing."

As we made our way back down the road, hand in hand, I noticed that the level of water in the river had gone down. In the distance, cries rang out, some of despair, some of confusion or loss...or terror. Some died abruptly.

"Can we escape?"

Neither mother nor father said anything and my heart sank. It could not be over, could it?

"There must be a way," I said.

Father shushed me and his rejection stung. I tried to pull my hand out of his, but he strengthened his grip. It hurt, but I kept silent.

We continued, our pace slow. I thought of my friends. Halianne, Virta, and Targatar. My heart skipped a beat at the thought of Targatar. We had made plans to meet this afternoon, at the foot of the waterfall. I wondered where the three of them were at this moment and if they were safe.

Just yesterday, Targatar had given me a bouquet of vernal flowers. It was beautiful, combining orange, white, and yellow. Mostly yellow, my favorite color.

For a moment, I considered asking my parents to go back home, to grab the bouquet hidden under my bed.

The bouquet...

Given to me by...I couldn't remember.

I stopped—fought against my father's pull—and looked back toward the village.

"It's so small," I whispered. So vulnerable.

The mist around it looked thicker, and angrier somehow, moving faster, devouring grass, flowers, and trees, roads, fences, and houses.

Sister's fingers squeezed mine, and I let father lead me along.

The hall rose ahead and I looked up but only saw the white barrier behind it, over it. I had expected to see something of beauty there, but there was nothing. I had expected to hear something as well, but it was eerily silent, with the exception of the random cry and the constant humming.

I continued to stare into the haze and knew that up there, somewhere, something red stood, looking down on us, standing guard over us. A statue of Shillis, the Red Lady.

But only an echo of crimson lingered in the fog.

"She abandoned us," I said.

My parents didn't say anything, continued to walk.

My eyes returned to the hall, to the many memories I had of the place, of playing hide-and-seek with sister in the main room, crouching between columns or in the shadows of the dais, behind the chairs, although we would get scolded if we got caught. I thought of the room at the end of the dark corridor. I thought of the Sentinel lying there.

The Sentinel, inert, paralyzed. An idea formed.

"What about the knife?" I asked.

I grabbed mother's arm, tugged on it until she looked at me.

"Mother, what about the knife?"

She looked at me, and blinked, and smiled, as if she had forgotten I was there, as if she was relieved that I was. "What do you mean?" she asked.

"The knife. It keeps the Sentinel paralyzed, right? It stops his powers. So I don't know, could it stop this thing?"

Mother frowned, looked at father, then back at me. "I don't know," she said. "Maybe not stop it, but possibly give us a way out." She nodded to herself. "Yes, it could work."

The four of us stood in front of the Sentinel. The man hadn't moved and the dagger still protruded from his chest. This close, the weapon looked unwieldy and crude. It had no cross-guard and its blade didn't reflect the light. Its surface was a dull silver, jagged, and something about it felt wrong. It made me regret bringing it up.

"Are you ready?" asked father.

Mother nodded.

"Will he wake up?" I asked.

"It's possible," mother said. "The three of us will leave, and your father will follow as soon as he can."

"Can I change my mind?" I asked. "I don't think this is a good idea anymore."

Mother smiled briefly. "There is no other option, Sirka. Yours is the only one, our last chance."

Father took a step forward and grabbed the hilt with both of his hands. He inhaled deeply and pulled. The dagger came out easily and father stumbled backward. The Sentinel gasped and started to flail, as if he was drowning in deep water. By pure mishap, one of his hands grabbed mother's arm. She tried to back away, but his grip was strong.

"Go," she said. "Ralka, take the children and leave. Now!"

The Sentinel rolled over, toppling off the side of the table, pulling mother to the floor.

"Girls, follow me," father said.

"No!" I yelled, dashing toward mother, but father caught me, dragged me away. As he did, my gaze crossed with the Sentinel's. Insanity, confusion, and pain danced in his eyes. I stopped struggling and let father carry me out of the room, through the corridor, the empty main room, and out through the back door. He put me down as soon as we were outside, setting sister beside me.

She looked awful, as if she had been starved for several days. Her cheekbones stood out, her eyes hid behind black rings, and her hair, her lovely red hair, lay flat against her skull like dried twigs.

The change had happened so swiftly.

"Your mother is more than capable of fending for herself," father said, but the tears in his eyes made it hard for me to believe him. "Remember that she's the one who stopped him in the first place. Let's go."

Sister took hold of my hand and it felt as if I was holding a cube of ice. I wondered what she was feeling, couldn't help worrying for her.

We followed father as he headed east. We passed in front of a house and I couldn't recollect who lived there. I searched for someone, anyone, but only saw the living wall of fog.

"Where is everyone?" I asked as we crossed a narrow bridge. It rose over the river before diving down between two white blossoming cherry trees. I kept squeezing sister's hand. I suspected that there was another bridge down the river, somewhere beyond the mist, but I wasn't able to visualize it.

Father ignored my question, instead concentrating on where we were going. It wasn't far. We passed the cherry trees and halted, the thick wreathing barrier looming in front of us, over us. It stirred and churned, and moved, getting closer.

"It's like it's alive," I said.

Strange low snarls came from it, like a mad dog I remembered from…I didn't know from where, just that it had been sick with disease and that it had to be killed.

"Stand back," father said, lifting the dagger. "Let's hope this works."

I stood transfixed, feelings of excitement and hope battling panic and trepidation.

Father lunged forward, bringing the blade down in an arc. The wall awoke and dove to meet him but veered away suddenly, seemingly afraid of the knife, or unable to come near it. The swing missed, leaving father off-balance. He hacked again, this time faster and with more purpose.

The crystal blade cut deeply into the barrier. Father added his second hand to the pommel and pushed the dagger down, opening a long vertical gash. Filaments of mist flogged away from the opening. Although it didn't make a sound, I knew the wall was in agony.

"Now!" father yelled, his voice galvanizing me into action.

I wrapped an arm around sister and pulled her forward. Father stepped aside, encouraging us to move faster. I was amazed at the size of the fissure; it had doubled already.

A flash of light passed through the barrier, blinding me momentarily. It was accompanied by a loud crack, so loud that sister and I found ourselves on the ground, arms over our heads.

"Quickly!" father howled. "It's closing!"

Without thinking, I grabbed sister by the waist and threw her forward. I tripped with the effort and when I lifted my head, the opening had shrunk considerably.

But sister...she was on the other side. I smiled at her and she stared back at me, tears running down her cheeks. Behind her, I saw a bare land, brown dirt, where nothing grew. What had I done? Where had I sent her?

"I love you." Her words drifted through just as the gash closed completely.

"I love you, sis," I yelled, knowing that it was too late.

A shadow appeared above me. Father, blade in hand, swung and slashed at the wall. The living fog retreated briefly, then flared. Once again, a deafening snap followed the white burst, so loud that I thought my eardrums would explode.

I grabbed my head and rolled into a ball. A hand took hold of my shoulder and shoved me aside. I found myself sprawled under one of the cherry-blossom trees. Panicked, I pushed myself up and turned toward my father.

My heart skipped a beat as I saw him on his knees, holding the crystal dagger over his head, mist flowing over him, around him, encasing him.

"Father!" I yelled.

He heard me and looked at me. "Go to your mother!"

He drove the blade above his head. The attack pushed the barrier farther up, but wisps of mist on the ground moved in and closed around one of his feet, crawled quickly up his leg, devouring it. Then the white mist swiftly absorbed the rest of him, leaving nothing behind.

The dagger fell to the ground, cleaving through the living miasma. I was alone, didn't remember wielding the weapon, but knew that my sister was on the other side, safe. Somehow.

I took a step forward, reaching toward the strange knife...but had to retreat. The barrier dove down, engulfing the weapon yet not able to touch it, forming an impenetrable cocoon around it.

My upper lip trembled uncontrollably. Tears blurred my sight. Confusion assaulted my mind.

A terrible emptiness tore at me from the inside. Although safe, I had lost my sister...and someone else...someone important, but whom I couldn't remember.

The barrier wafted closer, sucking in a cluster of sunny dandelions. I took a step back, jumped when a branch caressed me behind the ear. I turned, passed between the cherry blossoms, made my way across the bridge, stopped on the other side and looked back.

Sister was out there, on the other side of the wall. I missed her already, missed her small fingers in mine, missed her noises, missed her dancing hair and her weird, mismatched eyes.

I turned around, rushed back toward the hall and the only person left to me.

Mother gasped when I stepped between the hanging drapes in the small room. She jumped to her feet and came to me, hugged me.

"I love you so much," she said, as if she knew exactly what I needed. She looked over my shoulder. "Are you alone?"

I nodded.

She hesitated, not wanting to ask.

"Sister is free," I said. "She made it through."

Mother sighed and smiled briefly. Then she hugged me again, burying my face in her shoulder. I closed my eyes, welcoming her hand rubbing my back. "I'm so sorry. Come, come here with me."

As we stepped deeper in the room, I noticed that she wasn't alone. The Sentinel sat on the floor, his back against the table where he had lain not that long ago. I steeled myself, unwilling to follow, knowing that this individual was one of those responsible for the destruction of my village, of my family, of my life.

"You don't have to worry," mother said. "We wait together."

She guided me to a spot across from the man. We sat down together, her arm around my shoulders, my head against her chest.

The Sentinel looked awful. Dark blue pockets hung under his eyes. Long wrinkles plastered his forehead and the corners of his eyes. Stubs of a white beard decorated his lower cheeks and chin. Cracks of crusty blood tore at his lips.

"What did you do to us?" I asked. My words didn't contain the spite I wished they had. I didn't have the energy.

"Me?" he said, his voice just as spent as he looked. "Nothing. I did nothing to you." He laughed, and the high-pitched sound quickly turned into a gurgle. "But the others, they are removing you from history. And with you, me as well."

I looked at mother. "It's true," she said.

"What does he mean?"

"No one will remember us," mother said. "It will be like we never existed, like this village was never here."

"That's impossible!"

"It is possible," said the Sentinel.

"Do something then! Stop it, if you're so powerful."

"I'm here," mother said. "Think of me, of your sister."

I did, because anything else I tried to remember pulled at my mind and brought flashes of pain.

The man shook his head and there was pain there too, regret possibly. "I can't. Once the incantation has begun, nothing can reverse it. Within the bubble, I am like you. Without power."

I thought of sister and how cold her skin had been. Was that what had been happening to her as well? Was she like this man? Was she... one of them?

I studied the man and was surprised at how vulnerable he looked. He was broken, both in body and in mind, but just like us nonetheless.

"Do you have a family?" I asked.

The Sentinel's chin rested against his chest. "I do. A wife with whom I've shared my life for more than sixteen years. A daughter and son, her close to your age, I imagine. Him, a bit younger."

Like sister and me.

"I'm sorry," I said.

"That is kind."

"What are their names?"

At this, he looked up, a weak smile playing on his lips. "Silim and Galram," he said. "My daughter and my son. Laria, their mother."

"And you?"

He hesitated, suddenly uncertain. "Why do you ask?"

"It is only us now. Me, my mother, and you."

My explanation seemed to satisfy him. "I'm Dalgaram," he said. "And I'm the one who is sorry, deeply sorry."

Mother pulled me closer and wrapped me up in both arms.

"I'm so proud of you," she whispered in my ear.

I welcomed the words, let them sink in, bathed in their love.

Suddenly, the walls shook and moaned and cracked. The wails and screeches, easy to ignore before, were now too loud to be denied. I looked up and saw long tendrils of white mist infiltrating our room, taking hold of the roof and then wrenching it away from us. A deafening din followed...resonances of destruction, reverberations of annihilation.

The sounds of the end.

Mother turned my face toward her chest, hiding everything from me. She swaddled me with her arms, with her love.

There was only us now.

"I love you," she whispered in my ear.

"I love you, mother," I said.

And somewhere far, there was sister. Safe, I hoped. Reborn, I wished.

Madovic opened his eyes. He felt muzzy and depleted, as if he had performed a demanding act or woken up from a long slumber. Or both. He sat crossed-legged at the edge of a cliff, floating just above the ground. A glow exuding from the symbols on his forearms faded away.

He noticed a tube container resting on the ground in front of him. He picked it up, pulled out the parchment inside, and unrolled it.

You have reached the end of your pilgrimage. Well done.
Return to Tar Halia.
-Zil

Madovic put the scroll back in its case and looked up. He wasn't alone. A large detachment of his order stood around him, all of them awakening like he had. Closer, one of their Sages, Rhahas, was staring at him.

"It is done, then?" he asked.

The Sage's forearms had also been shining.

"It is so," Madovic answered. "Let's be on our way."

He showed the scroll case to support his words. Rhahas, much younger, nodded. It was understood that although Rhahas was a Sage, Madovic led their contingent.

"Prepare to depart," Madovic announced to the others.

As they prepared for the return home, he took a moment to study their surroundings. A wide barren area stretched ahead. There was a dry waterfall and river, which had once run between two high escarpments. It was easy to imagine beauty dwelling in this place in a past long forgotten. Even though there were no signs of life, Madovic felt uneasy, as if something was amiss. He sent out a few scouts to inspect the area.

They returned promptly. None had anything to report, except one.

"You should come," the scout said simply.

Madovic, Rhahas, and three others followed the scout, who led them down into the ravine, along the river, and farther to the east, where the two rocky facades opened up to rolling plains. Here, green grass sprinkled with yellow dandelions, golden shrubs, and white blooming trees replaced the dry and lifeless dirt.

"It is just beyond," said the scout, pointing to a high bluff.

As they reached the top, a crystal-clear lake was revealed, its shores a multicolored collection of spring blossoms. A small figure knelt by the water in between two bushes. A young girl.

"You spoke to her?" Madovic asked.

"No," the scout said. "I thought it best if you did."

Indeed, even from this far away, Madovic felt that the girl was out of the ordinary. He called upon one of his sigils and his vision changed and adapted. As it did, energy started to appear around the girl. At first, only one strand extended out of her, as it should be, but then a second, and a third. The bright filaments multiplied until the small figure was completely surrounded by them, barely perceptible in their center.

"What's wrong with her?" asked Rhahas by his side.

Madovic basked in the sight for a moment longer, then reverted his vision back to normal. "Nothing's wrong," he said. "We found a prodigy."

Without waiting, he floated down toward the lake, landing a few feet behind the girl.

Even though he didn't make a sound, she turned at his approach. Behind odd and drifting fiery hair, her eyes were full of tears.

"Are you alone?"

She nodded. Still, Madovic called upon his sigils and performed a scan of the surroundings. For as far as he could reach, the only signs of life he sensed were the other Sentinels. No wildlife. Strange.

"What is your name?" he asked.

She studied him and even though she was but a child, possibly five or six, Madovic felt that she was defying him somehow. She wasn't as young as they usually were when recruited, but still, he extended his hand to her.

She didn't take it right away. Instead, she looked toward the lake, as if pondering her decision, or saying goodbye to someone. Then she turned his way and reached out.

"I'm Shéana," she said.

S.C. Eston

STEVE C. ESTON has been a lover of the fantastical and the scientific since he was a young boy. He wrote his first story by hand while still in elementary school — a five-page story about a tiger-masked ninja fighting mystical monsters that included his own illustrations. When not spending time with his family, Steve makes time for his numerous hobbies, which include reading (and hoarding) books, listening to music, playing video games, watching movies, making puzzles, and playing hockey and tennis. He also loves to travel and developed an obsession with New Zealand after traveling there in 2015.

www.sceston.com

If you liked this short story and would like to learn more about Shéana, look for "The Stranger of Ul Darak", the first installment in *The Lost Tyronian Archives*.

Madame Beauvary's Curio Shop

By Angela Wren

The Village of Beauregard, 1983

THERE WAS SOMETHING DECIDEDLY ODD about Madame Beauvary, Alice Tomlinson concluded as she gazed out the window of La Vielle à Roue, the local bar and restaurant.

"Not least your name, nor its spelling," she muttered as she ripped her croissant into three before devouring a chunk of the pastry. Wiping her fingers on the small serviette Eric had delivered to the table along with her meagre breakfast, she focused her attention on the activity across the road. Her wide coffee cup cradled in her hands, Alice watched the sprightly octogenarian – was she really that old? – move bits and pieces of stock out onto the pavement.

The lifting and shifting complete, Madame Beauvary straightened her back and paused momentarily.

"And that's just what I mean," Alice whispered. "That pose. There's something not quite right about it." Her head on one side, Alice observed Madame Beauvary as she strode back into her shop. "Exactly how old are you?" She took another sip of her lukewarm coffee. Her glance shifted to the old-fashioned, black-painted wooden shop frontage with faded gold lettering above the substantial front window – Brocante du Beauvary. Alice smiled as she recalled the sparkling blue and white stoned brooch that Madame Beauvary always wore to secure one of her many silk scarves about her neck. She wondered which came first, the double 'bb' of the jewelry or the name of the business.

"Another coffee, Alice?" Eric called across the space as he reached for a fresh cup and saucer.

Alice nodded, collected her empty breakfast crockery together and moved to the bar. "Nothing ever changes here does it, Eric?" The pots were deposited on the counter with a rattle.

"Not really," he said over the whoosh of the coffee machine as it delivered another café au lait.

"Just like Madame Beauvary," Alice said as she leaned back against the bar, her gaze firmly fixed on the large window and the view of the shop owner winding out the canvas awning to protect her goods from the sun.

"I've been here for two months now, and Madame Beauvary does exactly the same thing every day. Does she ever sell anything from that business of hers?" Alice blinked away the assault on her sight of the almost neon green of Madame Beauvary's top for the day which neither matched nor complemented the lurid purple of her skirt.

Alice turned to face Eric. "She even wears the same sort of clothes, which she changes regularly, of course."

Eric smiled. "Perhaps her dress is a little eccentric, but Madame Beauvary has been here a very long time," he said. "Well, for as long as I can remember. Some say that she bought that place just after the war. With so many displaced people and things, I suppose she thought she could make a decent living back then." He slid the fresh coffee across the counter.

"Thanks," said Alice, adding some sugar and stirring. "Hmm, yes, I can see why she might take on house clearances, buying and selling and so on. But it all looks very mundane, old-fashioned stuff to me."

"Have you been inside?"

Alice shook her head.

"What I do know is that you can find anything in that place." He glanced at the light fittings on the walls around the recently decorated room. Alice followed his gaze.

"From Madame Beauvary's brocante?" She took a sip of her coffee.

Eric nodded as he turned his attention to his washing up. "Those two on the far wall and her place was the only one that had them."

Alice looked at each of the four sconces. Yes, she thought, they are a perfect match and they look to be 1930s in style and design. And probably genuine. "Hmm, I might pay Madame Beauvary a visit," she said before taking a gulp of the sweet, milky drink.

It was a week before Alice managed to free herself from her job as Events Manager at the château for a couple of hours. Leaving her shared office in the west wing behind, she skipped down the stairs and out into the early afternoon sunshine. She took the path around the house and through the carefully laid out gardens. The flower beds were a riot of pink, purple, yellow, and pale green. As she walked, she breathed in and relished the fresh scent of new flowers and mown grass. It was a twenty-minute stroll across the estate to the edge of the village. Turning onto rue du Onze Novembre, the main street that ran through the centre of the village, she hurried her pace. Her anticipation at what she might find in the bizarre little shop pushed her on for the next hundred meters or so.

She paused at the narrow doorway. In front of her, a flight of stairs stretched up to the second floor, each step containing books that effectively halved the space for the customer to tread. The walls of the small entrance were covered with pictures and a large green urn stood at the foot of the stairs.

Alice took a deep breath and stepped into the main area on her left. Inside, it was crammed full with every possible kind of household item. Numerous light fittings were hanging from every centimeter of ceiling. The walls were covered with shelves that looked fit to crash down on each other and, on the floor space in between, there were cabinets jam-packed with stuff. Alice held her breath. The slightest disturbance or ripple of air might cause any one of the stacked piles of crockery and nick-nacks to topple and smash to the ground. She nervously pulled the ponytail of her dark red, unruly hair forward across her right shoulder.

In the middle of the room, Madame Beauvary sat at a tiny counter with no space for a cash till. She was surrounded by her merchandise. Had she not been speaking on the phone – a tall wooden mouthpiece and earpiece connected by a cable dating from the early 1920s – Alice might have mistaken her for a display item!

Alice smiled as she took in the detail of the vision that was Madame Beauvary. The skin of every finger of each hand was starved of light and sight by numerous rings and fingerless gloves. Each wrist was equally encumbered by a weight of jewelry that rattled and jingled as she moved the telephone mouthpiece in support of her argument. Around her neck were the usual swathe of floaty scarves, secured by a couple of stoned and sparkling pins. Definitely fake, thought Alice. The crowning note, Alice noticed, for the rainbow displayed by the clothes and accessories was the bright blood-red of Madame Beauvary's fingernails and matching lipstick.

Alice made to step past the counter area. "Do take your time browsing, Madame," said the shop owner, clutching the mouthpiece to her ample chest. "I'll be with you as soon as I can."

Before Alice had chance to thank her, Madame Beauvary was continuing her seemingly one-sided conversation. She certainly never once paused to listen to the voice at the other end of the line within Alice's hearing. Negotiating prices was obviously of more importance than attending to a real and present customer.

Alice meandered away from the owner and moved on toward the back of the shop where every millimeter of space on yet more shelves was obliterated by stock – some of it genuinely old, some of it new, some of it rubbish, and some of it only of value to a previous owner who had cherished it.

"Who wants a chipped and worn earthenware meat plate that size?" Alice let out a sigh. Continuing her browsing, a small scent bottle perched on the edge of an upper shelf caught her eye. The glass was white, opaque, and decorated on the shoulders with tiny pink flowers and a garland of pale green leaves. She gingerly removed the stopper. It was intact. Alice took out her loupe to get a closer look.

"Unusual," she commented to herself.

"A lot of my pieces are, Madame."

Alice jumped but managed to keep a firm grip on the bottle. Madame Beauvary stood at the side of her smiling, her heavy make-up seeping into the creases of skin around her mouth.

"French," she offered at last. "Mid-nineteenth century and probably made in Paris."

"Not Italian, then?" Alice put her lens to her eye again and scanned the decoration. "Paste," she said. Turning the item upside down she examined the base. "And hardly any evidence of wear," she said replacing her glass in the pocket of her linen jacket. And made last month, she thought to herself as she forced a smile for the shop owner's benefit.

Madame Beauvary took a step back. "I see you know your antiques and collectables. Are you a dealer, Madame?"

"Not anymore," said Alice choosing not to correct the assumption. And anyway, a trained auctioneer and valuer's work was not so very far removed from that of a bona fide dealer. "I work at the château, now."

"Ah! Of course, you must be Monsieur Tomlinson's daughter. Are you here on his behalf?"

Alice replaced the scent bottle. "Yes, I am and no, I'm not here on Dad's behalf. I just wanted to have a look inside your amazing shop. I often see you opening up in a morning whilst I'm having a coffee at the bar. Most days I pop into La Vielle à Roue on my way to work."

"Ah, I see. And is there anything in particular that you would like me to find for you?"

Alice shook her head. "No, I don't think so." The picture of her mother's bracelet popped into her mind and for a fleeting second she thought she might explain. But as she stepped away and moved back toward the entrance, she told herself, no. That will never be found, she thought. It was lost too long ago.

At the doorway, on an impulse, she turned. "Silver," she said. "If you come across any decent silver jewelry, I might be interested."

Madame Beauvary was across the shop in only two or three strides.

"Any particular style or period? With or without stones?"

Alice took half a step back. "It must be English silver. Fully hallmarked." She moved outside, glad to be out of the place. The sun seemed unusually strong considering it was the end of March and just a few days before Easter. Alice squinted; perhaps it was just the contrast between the lack of light in the shop and the brightness of the spring afternoon. Whatever it was, the sun and clear air had lost its interest. Her mood had changed. As it always did when she thought about her mother. Barely looking right or left she moved down the street toward her rented rooms above the boulangerie.

A few minutes later, Alice climbed the stairs to her third-floor apartment. As she pushed the key in the lock she felt tears welling in her eyes. She blinked them away and let the door slam shut behind her.

"Ridiculous," she said as she kicked off her shoes. Her bag and jacket were flung on the sofa. Sniffing, she marched across to the French windows and opened them. Her violin and bow were still on the stand from the previous evening. Without conscious thought, she picked them up and began to play. Sheet music was not necessary. Every note was imprinted on her heart. As each one was angrily forced from the instrument, her feelings for her mother were steadily exorcized. The loss she had incomprehensibly suffered at too young an age dissipated into a distant recess in her memory – there to remain until she unlocked it again.

As she commenced the third repeat, her eyes slowly closed and she finally lost herself to the melody. The lilting notes drifting out into the cooling air and across the river Buevron and the land that once belonged to the ducs de Berry.

The final note delivered to her audience of flora and fauna, she replaced the instrument and stared out across the rolling countryside. A light tap on the door, followed by a familiar voice, interrupted her calm.

"Alice?"

"Come in, Dad, the door's open." She quickly scooped up her bag and jacket.

"Are you alright?" Peter Tomlinson stepped into the room and stood behind the sofa. "*The Rusty Knight.* It's a long time since I've heard you play that piece."

"It's *Cavallaria Rusticana*, Dad, as well you know," Alice replied as she took her bag and jacket to the bedroom. Walking back into the living space she looked at her father, a half-smile on her face.

"I know," said Peter. "But I also know what it means to you. Who has upset you?"

Alice flopped down on the sofa. "No one. Well, me actually. I just went into the brocante in the village and for some stupid reason I thought I might find Mum's... And that got me thinking and... It doesn't matter."

Peter nodded. "But you're OK now?"

"Yes, I'm fine, thanks."

"So, you've met Madame Beauvary?" He moved over to the window, leaned against the frame and ran his hand through his head of thick black hair peppered with silver.

Alice nodded.

"And?" He cleared his throat. "Did you make yourself known to her?"

Alice looked at her dad. "Not exactly. Why?"

"Nothing," said Peter as he shoved his hands in his trouser pockets and meandered across to sit beside her. "I sometimes do a bit of business with her."

Alice stared at her dad. "Business?" She frowned. "What kind of business?"

"She finds fittings for me when I'm renovating a property. She also tells me about any period or ornamental architectural features she comes across when she does her house clearances. And, occasionally, if I need to dress a newly decorated or renovated room or property, Madame B will let me borrow some of her stock for the photos. Madame B found that blue and white dinner service I used for the publicity shots when I did that barn conversion last year. It's a mutual benefit kind of thing."

"Not quite an above-board working relationship?" Alice sat up straight.

Peter grinned.

"Well?"

"Everything is on the level," Peter said putting his hand on his daughter's and squeezing it. "Madame B drives a hard bargain, though. But I give as good as I get and her shop always gets a mention in any publicity. Stop worrying. Now," Peter stood up. "Have you still got time to meet my new clients?"

Alice nodded.

"OK. We need to get a move on. I'm meeting them for an apéritif," said Peter as he strode across to the door. "And, remember, I need you there because of your experience as a valuer."

It was the Friday after Easter when Alice saw Madame Beauvary again. Her shop had remained firmly closed throughout the week with only a small wooden sign hanging on the shutter doors saying 'Acheter Aujourd'hui'.

What Alice couldn't understand was how sellers got access to a closed shop when Madame Beauvary was buying if she wasn't there. But then, on each morning the sign had been present, no sellers had called and Alice had been left staring at an empty pavement. The only conclusion was that the sign signified that Madame Beauvary was purchasing elsewhere.

Her day at the château passed quickly and Alice was glad to get away just after five that afternoon. She walked across the estate and into the village. She needed some flour, eggs and salad from the tiny general store, and some fresh bread from Gérard. She thought she might treat herself to some of his macarons, too.

"Assuming there are any left," she muttered as she strode past the church and down toward the centre of the village. Turning the corner and looking ahead, she saw that the brocante was now open. Her pace quickened.

Drawing level with the front window she glanced at three paintings that she was certain had not been on display before. Two were sitting, one resting on the top of the frame of the other, in an old rattan chair that was regularly out on display. The third, propped up against the window, she dismissed as an ugly daub.

"I wonder what happened to the doll." Alice eyed the uppermost piece of art that had replaced the child's beautifully dressed toy. The blue ground was a perfect backdrop for the rich creamy white of the flowers and dark green of the foliage that seemed to sit in suspended animation at the center of the canvas. The brushstrokes were confident. The changes of direction deliberate to catch the fall of light so that the viewer saw variance in the shade of the background rather than a flat color. Searching the corners of the picture, Alice could see no signature. She took a step back.

"I see the little Dutch oil has caught your eye, Mademoiselle Tomlinson."

Alice looked in the direction of the voice. Today, Madame Beauvary, framed by the doorway of her shop, looked a living and breathing example of the Pop Art movement. Her pale-blue kitten heels screamed in contrast at the thick brown stockings wrinkling around her ankles. The fuchsia-pink skirt and ocher-yellow top, finished off with yet another swathe of scarves, made Alice's eyes dance. She had never suffered from migraines, but she felt sure one might be on the way if she did not shift her gaze back to the soothing blue and white of the painting.

"Yes," she said after a moment. "I was wondering if you would mind if I looked at it in the sunlight rather than the shadow of your awning."

Madame Beauvary smiled. "Of course, Mademoiselle. Please take your time."

Alice carefully lifted the artwork from its resting place and moved out into the bright light. The picture was transformed. The various shades of blue and gray used to create the background came alive, and in the petals of the flowers, Alice could see tiny flecks of pale yellow that added depth and shape, similar to the dark gray touches for the foliage. She turned her attention to the back. On one strut of the stretcher was a mark. The framer, she told herself. To the left was an old paper label that had yellowed with age, but the text was still readable.

"So, this has been in an exhibition in Lyon," she said looking directly at the shop owner.

"Yes, Mademoiselle. And I have the full provenance if you would like to see it."

Alice noted the complete lack of expression on Madame Beauvary's face. You know exactly what you're doing, she thought. Alice began to scrutinize the frame and the back of the picture.

"And the artist, Madame Beauvary? If you have the full provenance you must know the creator."

"I believe it to be a Johannes Hoedemaker," she said. "He usually signs his works JAH and sometimes as JanH."

"And is this one signed?"

Madame Beauvary frowned. "Unfortunately not. But it has been on exhibition with some of his other works."

And unless it is listed in the catalogue raisonné, thought Alice, then such an association is nothing more than that.

"I see." Alice returned the picture to its resting place on the chair and took a couple of steps back.

"I do like the subject and the colors," she said, visualizing, at the same time, the wall in her apartment on which it might hang. But, she reminded herself, appearing too eager never made any sense.

"For a small fee I can bring the piece to you, if you wish."

Alice looked at the shop owner. The lipstick of her blood-red mouth was stretched into a thin line. The brown eyes were steady and unblinking.

"I'm not sure I understand, Madame."

"Not everyone has the ability to visualize an artwork in situ. I'm able to provide advice and guidance."

Alice smiled. "I see," she said. "And how small is the small fee, Madame Beauvary?"

"Ten Francs an hour."

The response was so rapid and enunciated without a flinch that Alice was taken aback.

"Oh! Erm. Right. I think I'll leave it for the moment and think about it some more."

Madame Beauvary nodded. "The price to buy is seven hundred and fifty Francs, Mademoiselle."

Alice nodded. "Thank you." She hurried away down the street, mentally calculating the cost in sterling as she strode along.

Later that evening, Alice walked into the spare room of her apartment and flicked on the bare bulb hanging from the center of the ceiling. Glancing up at the garish beam of light she wondered if Madame Beauvary might have an appropriate fitting amongst her collection.

"But what would be the point?" Alice shook the idea away. She would only be in this place for another month or so. Once her dad had got his current project completed she would be moving into a newly refitted and decorated home of her own on the edge of the village, overlooking the river.

"That's the time to buy lights and shades and stuff," she said as she stepped between the numerous cardboard boxes on the floor. A quick check of the labels on each one and she realized the container she needed was on the unmade bed. A further search led her to one at the back and inside were a selection of books on art. Hefting the box off the thin mattress she carried it through to the sitting room.

"I think it's going to be a long night," she mused as she selected a substantial tome and pulled it out.

Despite the lateness of the hour the previous evening when Alice finally went to bed, she was up at dawn the following morning. Still in her navy-spotted pajamas, she was settled at the kitchen breakfast bar with a cup of half-drunk coffee, a piece of abandoned toast, a selection of books on art, and a notebook and pen. As she read, she jotted down helpful information.

Stretching and yawning, she heard the clock on the church tower ponderously strike eight. In a frenzy of activity, Alice shoved her notes in her bag, collected the remains of her breakfast and dumped the pots in the sink. If she was going to the library in Blois, she needed to be at the bus stop by the bridge in ten minutes flat.

Alice plonked herself down on her dad's sofa. "It's been a long day," she said.

"And the pleasure of this unexpected visit is because?" Peter settled himself in his armchair with a large glass of beer.

Alice grimaced. "Yes, sorry about that, but I've been at the library all day today, and I need a favor."

Peter took a long draught of his beer. "I'm listening."

Where to begin? Alice wondered. Probably with as little information as possible, she silently answered her question. Lifting her gaze from the oriental rug, Alice looked at her dad.

"Madame Beauvary has got a painting that I'm interested in. I saw it outside her shop yesterday. And I was wondering. Well, I was hoping that you might be able to borrow it from her using your agreement so that I could get a better look at it."

Peter took another drink. "A better look in search of?"

Alice frowned. Why do you always do that, Dad? OK, time to be almost honest.

"In search of a signature. I think one may be hidden behind the frame."

Peter nodded. "Uh-huh. Which means you must think the painting is valuable."

"I wouldn't say that exactly, Dad."

"Then what would you say? Exactly?" Peter put his glass down on the coffee table.

Alice cleared her throat. "That there is a question of authenticity that I'm trying to resolve."

"Uh-huh. In whose favor?"

A cheery response of 'Madame Beauvary's, of course', popped into Alice's mind. She decided to dial back on the positivity.

"Ultimately, Madame Beauvary will benefit, if I'm right," she said, carefully choosing her words. After all, she thought, whatever the final outcome of her research, Madame Beauvary could still sell the painting. It was just a question of the level of benefit. Alice waited for her father to respond.

"OK," he said at last after draining his glass. "As it happens, I've finished the ground floor apartment anyway, and I could start dressing those rooms for some photos. I'll call in and see Madame B. Which painting is it?"

"Thanks, Dad. There's a label on the back from an exhibition in Lyon. The title on there is *White Flowers* and, according to my research, that exhibition took place in 1938. So, I expect that the picture was created around that time or a couple of years before."

Peter nodded. "I'll give you a ring at work when I've got it."

Alice stood. "Thanks, Dad."

The week and the work at the château dragged interminably for Alice. All she wanted were answers to all the unresolved questions surrounding the Hoedemaker picture. It was Thursday afternoon before the call from her father came through. At the earliest opportunity, she was out of the office, across the estate and hurrying along the street to her apartment. Running up the stairs, she saw her dad waiting on the landing, a rectangular brown paper parcel under his arm.

A broad grin on her face she unlocked the door. "Thanks, Dad. This is going to be a real discovery if I'm right."

Peter smiled and followed her in. "And you are, usually," he said.

Alice abandoned her jacket on the back of the sofa and dropped her bag on the floor. She cleared the pots from the breakfast bar and wiped it down. Covering the space with a couple of clean dishtowels, she nodded to her father.

Peter placed the parcel on the worktop and began to untie the string. Alice rubbed her hands together and watched as the picture was revealed.

"Flowers!" Peter said as he peeled back the paper. "It's a bit chocolate-box, but it looks quality to me."

Alice wasn't listening. She was concentrating on a detailed examination of the surface of the painting. Turning it this way and that to capture the light. Finally convinced there was no more detail to see, she flipped the artwork over and examined the back. Placing it face down, she reached into a drawer and selected a small screwdriver. Releasing the screws that held the stays for the canvas, she carefully lifted the painting out of the frame.

"You can get that back in place properly, can't you?"

"Of course, Dad. Don't fret." With the frame removed she placed it to one side. "OK, we really need to take some photos, Dad. I don't suppose you've got your camera?"

"Right here," he said holding up a small black camera bag. "Do you want me to do that?"

Alice nodded. For the next twenty minutes, as Alice positioned and re-positioned the picture, her dad took shot after shot, changing the reel of film twice.

"OK, that should be enough. Now, I just want to look at something here on the side of the stretcher." Alice moved across the room to her jacket and pulled her loupe out of the pocket. In a moment she was back behind the breakfast bar.

"Paint," she said as she moved onto another side of the stretcher. "Paint, Dad," she repeated having completed a magnified examination of all four sides of the stretcher.

Peter frowned. "I'm not following, sweetie. It's an oil painting; it's got to have paint."

Alice looked up and rolled her eyes. She offered her father the lens. "Yes," she said. "But this is evidence of an underneath layer of paint that is a completely different color. It's not the right paint."

Peter handed the glass back. "I see what you mean."

"This picture has been painted over something else." Alice picked up her lens and scanned the center of the canvas. "And what is even more interesting is that there are just visible traces of the canvas supplier. Look." She offered the glass to her dad.

Peter used the magnifying glass to scrutinize the back of the canvas. "No, I can't make it out. Have you got a torch?"

Alice scrabbled around in the cupboard under the sink. "Yes," she said straightening up. "But I've no idea if it works." She applied pressure to the switch. It shifted forward a fraction and then suddenly became free and the beam shone across the room. Alice directed the light onto the aged brown surface of the picture.

Peter studied what remained of the faded lettering. "I can make out a name, but it looks English to me."

Alice grinned. "Exactly!"

"And that means what?" Peter looked up.

"That the original artwork is not Hoedemaker's. It can't be. According to all the research I've done so far, there is no record of Hoedemaker being in England."

"Wait a minute, you've lost me now. Who's Hoedemaker?"

"Johannes Hoedemaker, an artist, was born in Amsterdam in 1894 and died in France in 1968. He was." She stopped herself. "Well, I suppose I'd better put this back," she said picking up the canvas and slipping it into the frame.

Peter took a step back. "Hoedemaker was what?"

Alice paused and looked up. She took a breath and kept her voice steady. "He was not a particularly sought-after artist in his own country. It was only when he came to France in the last few months of the 1930s that his work first began to be recognized."

"And the rest?"

Alice looked her dad in the eye. He was wearing his don't-even-think-about-trying-to-get-away-with-it, look. She'd seen it many times as a teenager and knew that it was always followed with a pointed statement. And three, four, five, she counted in her head.

"I can always do the same research myself," he said. "I have the capability, you know."

Alice sat down on a bar stool and sighed. "OK, you win," she said. "But I need to cross-check something at the library in Blois first. So, how about you and I return the picture to Madame Beauvary together after I've done that?"

Peter nodded. "That seems fair. But I'll take the painting with me."

Alice nodded and set to work getting the frame securely re-attached to the canvas.

It was after three before Alice could extricate herself from the work at the château. Once her colleague Sylvie was out of the way and ensconced in her employer's office, she picked up the phone and dialed the number of the gallery in Lyon. The conversation with the archivist was short and to the point. It provided one of the last pieces of the puzzle surrounding the painting.

Alice packed her papers in the drawer, locked it and left a note on Sylvie's desk. 'Left to meet Dad. See you tomorrow.'

The walk to the brocante was achieved in double-quick time. As she strode along the street she could see her father waiting for her. He was chatting to someone, Madame Beauvary she presumed, who must have been in the entrance to the shop. Alice hurried on.

"Madame Beauvary, Dad." Alice nodded to them both as she moved inside. Here two months and I've already picked up a French habit, she thought.

"I'm so glad you have returned. Peter tells me you are interested in my little Dutch oil." Madame Beauvary was her usual riot of color, but worn with a beaming smile.

Not at your price, thought Alice. "Yes, I'm quite intrigued by it," she said.

Peter attempted to put the picture in the only available space on the counter. The shop owner hurriedly moved things around to accommodate it. Alice removed the picture from its brown paper cover and propped it up.

"I want to start with the back of the picture," she said. "There are some important clues about the authenticity of this artwork there. I'm sure you will have noticed them, Madame." Alice turned to the shop owner. The smile was gone. The eyes were steady. The face, unmoving and pale, had the look of a Victorian death mask. Alice felt a shudder run down her spine.

"This frame does not appear to be the original one for the artwork. As you can see there are the remains of glue and brown paper that has been torn off the back." She glanced at Madame Beauvary. There was not a flicker of acknowledgement. "The label is a most important clue. You told me last week that you had the full provenance and I would quite like to see that. But, please, just listen for a moment."

Madame Beauvary gave a barely perceptible nod.

"I've done some research and I've spoken to the archivist at the gallery in Lyon. Yes, there was an exhibition in 1938 that featured the work of Johannes Hoedemaker, and there was a painting included called *White Flowers*. But this isn't it. The original painting of that name features roses. Some already arrayed in a vase that stands on a small table.

Other flowers and some secateurs are lying on the table beside the vase."

Alice paused, expecting Madame Beauvary to remonstrate. But there was nothing. Not even a glimmer of a change of expression. Interesting, she thought, but decided to continue.

"In addition, it was sold at the exhibition to a private collector. That's why I'm so curious to see your provenance, Madame Beauvary."

Without a word the shop owner disappeared behind her counter and, from a drawer, pulled out an old, worn ledger. She flicked through the pages.

"Ah! Here we are," she said at last as she checked the contents of a couple of pieces of paper clipped to the top of a page. "The bill of sale from the gallery in Lyon. I purchased this along with other contents as part of a house clearance in Blois, from a Monsieur Charles Bernier."

"And the name on the bill of sale from the gallery?" Peter asked.

Madame Beauvary glanced at her paperwork. "Monsieur Isidor Bernier. He was the grandfather of Monsieur Charles. I checked at the time of purchase." A faint smile of triumph crossed Madame Beauvary's face for the first time.

Alice nodded. "That's good," she said. "It establishes a direct link between the gallery, the picture and the person who sold you this canvas." She glanced at her dad and sighed.

"I have an idea that everything is not so straightforward, Alice. Is that right?"

"Hmm, yes. There's a problem with the size of this picture. According to my contact at the gallery in Lyon, the artwork documented as *White Flowers* is twice the size of this one." Alice left her statement hanging.

Peter frowned. "What are you saying, Alice? Do you think the frame could be from the original artwork, which has been cut down to fit this picture?"

Madame Beauvary was still unmoved.

"It's possible, Dad. It would explain the gallery label on the back of the frame. Unless that's a very clever fake. New owners do reframe artworks." Alice shook her head. "But that just doesn't add up, Dad. Does it? If you had an original artwork that you had reframed, wouldn't you make a point of keeping the relevant receipt or paperwork with that item?"

Peter shrugged. "Probably. Unless you wanted to pull a fast one and had copies made of the label and the paperwork. Then you'd have two apparently valuable artworks to sell."

"Yes, and I've seen that done before." Alice turned to the shop owner. "But it still leaves the question of the missing original artwork. Are you able to comment on that?"

Madame Beauvary cleared her throat. "I can only tell you what I know. This picture came to me as part of a house clearance in Blois. The provenance is what it is. I can't be held responsible for someone else's error."

"OK, that's true. And I'm not accusing you of anything, but there's also a problem with the actual age of this canvas. And, yes, the discoloring on the back here suggests that it is at least thirty or forty years old. But I've discovered that the material for this canvas came from England. If you look very carefully, you'll see the faint remains of a printed stamp, and the name is English."

Madame Beauvary tutted. "My eyes are not what they used to be," she said without expression or emphasis.

"From my research," Alice continued, "I can find no record of Johannes Hoedemaker working in, or visiting, England at any time during his life. If you consult the catalogue raisonné, you will find that no single work of art, in any medium, features any location in England. As Hoedemaker was principally a landscape artist with a particular interest in flora and fauna, who only worked here in France or Holland, I just think it's very odd that he should be using canvas sourced in Britain at the time that this painting was supposed to have been created."

Alice watched as the shop owner's shoulders stiffened slightly.

"The time that this painting was supposed to have been created," Madame Beauvary repeated as if the statement were something only to be spoken by rote.

Alice frowned. "Madame Beauvary, I'm simply pointing out to you that this picture, as pretty as it is, is unlikely to be a genuine Johannes Hoedemaker." She turned the picture over and gazed at the blue and white of the subject matter. "And the fact that there is no signature supports that."

The silence in the shop suddenly seemed oppressive. For the first time Alice noticed that there appeared to be the merest hint of a shadow of color under Madame Beauvary's heavy make-up.

"But that is only your opinion based on your research," she said.

"Of course," said Peter, a wide smile on his face. "But there is some good news, too. Isn't there, Alice?"

She shot her father a glaring stare. "Well, I wouldn't put it quite like that, Dad." She grimaced at Madame Beauvary. "But this picture does have more to tell us," she conceded.

"I think you'll be surprised."

"Yes! Thanks, Dad. I can explain." Alice felt the heat of her impatience creeping up her neck. "There's another possibility, Madame Beauvary. Johannes Hoedemaker had a daughter, Rosalie, who also painted. She studied fine arts in London and had a small number of artworks included in three exhibitions. Unfortunately, she died from a drug overdose just four years after her father's death. All of her known works, paintings, sketches and watercolors, were completed in London and along the south coast of England between 1963 and 1972. Like her father, she painted mostly landscapes; unlike her dad, she was the better artist. But she also created many works that featured flowers, in particular, roses."

Madame Beauvary grinned. "Her name, of course."

"That's right," said Alice.

"So you think Hoedemaker's daughter might be the artist? Interesting."

Alice crossed her arms and stared at the picture for a moment. "No, that's not what I'm saying. Underneath this expanse of blue and white oils is another picture. If you take it out of the frame, you will see there are flecks of paint in a completely different color scheme that have not been covered by this later piece of work. What I'm telling you is, there's another picture beneath this one that might be worth investigating. Whether that earlier piece of work connects to Hoedemaker, either father or daughter, is impossible to say without the appropriate analysis. But Rosalie did return to France for a short time in 1965 following a period in rehab. Did she bring some of her own canvasses with her and rework them?" Alice let out a heavy sigh before answering her own question. "I just don't know, Madame Beauvary. But it's possible, and you would need to consult an expert. I can make a recommendation if you wish."

"I see. And there will be a charge for that, I suppose."

Alice nodded. "And it won't be small."

"And you're certain this isn't the work of Johannes Hoedemaker?" She tapped the frame with a red-pointed forefinger.

"Yes, I am certain and I hope you didn't pay too much for it. Obviously, I'm no longer interested in buying the artwork. But, if you pursue the investigation, I would like to know the outcome. If you don't mind. And I would still be interested in hallmarked English silver if you come across any, if that helps."

Madame Beauvary's face relaxed into her unreadable saleswoman's expression. "Too bad," she said with a shrug. "Thank you for your information, Mademoiselle." She quickly collected the picture and its wrapping and disappeared toward the back of the shop.

Alice looked at her dad. "Did I say something wrong?"

Peter smiled. "Nothing important. She's lost a sale, and that's something she never likes to admit. Come on, I'll buy you a drink at the bar."

Just after six, Madame Beauvary began the second major ritual of her shop-filled day. A box of old photographs was retrieved from the mock-mahogany occasional table outside and deposited at the foot of the stairs. Next, the table was brought in and stood over it. The sizable free-standing globe dating from the early thirties was carried in and placed at the entrance to the main space. This was followed by the rattan chair containing only one painting. Finally, she brought in the child's pram and placed it behind the chair. Pulling the two full length shutters toward her, Madame Beauvary closed out the light on her emporium. With just enough space to spin around, she secured the shutters, closed the front door, locked it, and pushed the bolts across.

"I think the doll can go back outside tomorrow," she muttered as she carefully edged past the globe and the table to make her way up the stairs. She trudged up to the first floor with her large feet barely fitting on the narrow steps. On the landing, she paused to check that everything was in order. Mounting the second flight, she made her way to her rooms.

Entering her apartment, she slammed the door shut. This was her space. Here she could be herself, and the rest of the world could keep out.

As had become her habit, she moved to the elegant cabinet – walnut, inlaid, and a genuine antique – over by the window. From the silver platter, she picked up a cut-glass decanter of pastis from Marseille and poured a measure into a turn-of-the-century glass. Traipsing into the kitchen, she filled a small crystal jug with water and returned to the lounge to add a few drops to the glass.

"That Tomlinson woman is going to be trouble," she said eyeing her drink before taking a well-earned sip. "First she asks for English silver," she muttered as her forefinger skimmed the rim of the solid silver drinks tray. "Fully hallmarked, too." She cast a triumphal grin at the elegant piece before moving across the room.

On the gold brocade of the chaise longue, Madame Beauvary kicked off her kitten-heeled shoes. She stretched out her toes, uttering a gentle sigh of relief as she did so.

Another taste of the aniseed liqueur, and her left hand reached up to the front of her scalp, removed the blonde wig, and dropped it onto the stand that stood on a small table beside the chaise. The wig cap followed in the next second. And gradually, between recuperating tastes of the yellow indulgence, the scarves and pins were removed one by one. Setting the empty glass on the floor for a moment, Madame Beauvary took her talon-like fingers and scrubbed them through the short, gray, thinning hair that now only encompassed a circle around the sides of the head.

The skirt and top were the next items of clothing to be discarded. Encumbered only by the female-shaped theatrical bodysuit and the thick brown stockings, Michael Johnson stood up and got himself another drink.

"English silver," he said with a voice pitched at its born level of baritone. "Why would she be looking for English silver here in France?" He paused for a moment before adding a splash of water to the glass. "Why would anyone expect to find English silver here in this forsaken backwater?" Michael flopped down on the chaise, a deep frown on his forehead.

"And if she knows as much about English silver as she does about art, I might be done for." He shook his head. "Never for a moment thought she'd spot that fake!" He stretched out his legs and re-arranged the small bolster before knocking back the glassful of alcohol in one.

Angela Wren

Angela Wren is an actor and director at a theatre in Yorkshire, UK. An avid reader, she has always loved stories of any description. She writes the Jacques Forêt crime novels set in France and is a contributing author to the Miss Moonshine anthologies. Her short stories vary between romance, memoir, mystery and historical. Angela has had two one-act plays recorded for local radio.

www.angelawren.co.uk

As Flies to Wanton Boys

By Gianetta Murray

DEMI WAS CLEANING HOUSE as she always did this time of year, in anticipation of her daughter coming to stay. Which mostly meant giving orders to the help, an appellation she was sure the quality of their work did not warrant.

She was in the middle of an argument about the best solution for cleaning windows when there was a knock on the front door. In truth, it was more of a pounding, which gave Demi some idea who had come calling. She gave a resigned sigh and went to answer it. Even incompetent servants didn't deserve to face what was on the other side.

A chilly breeze snuck in when she opened the door, declaring winter was not quite over. Demi was surprised it hadn't been heated by the boiling rage of the enormous man facing her.

"Hello Zee," she intoned with a wave of her hand and as he strode past her into the house, "By all means, do come in."

"I told you this wouldn't end well!" her visitor turned and yelled, his curly black locks vibrating with indignation. "Why couldn't you have left well enough alone? What possessed you to do something so thoughtless and rash?"

Demi's shoulders slumped as her brother's verbal blows rained down on her, glad he was at least restraining his tendency to thunder. And she did, to some degree, deserve it.

But then she thought back to that fateful day in August of 1859 and straightened her back, her own temper asserting itself.

"I was angry! And frustrated! Seph was packing to leave once again, and I just couldn't bear it! Another six months of loneliness, of longing for my only child, a child that you and your stupid decrees take from me every single year."

Demi could feel the tears forming and fought to hold them back. Her brother wasn't one to be swayed by female sobbing, unless it was done by someone he was amorously pursuing. Still, he must have noticed her distress, because he sat her on a nearby chaise longue and his next words were more conciliatory.

"To go to her husband, Demi. Surely her husband has a right to spend time with her as well? And don't forget, she's my daughter, too."

Demi glanced up snarling at that. "Oh please. You know very well she isn't your daughter, you only claimed her to keep the peace. And that dour cadaver you forced her to marry is no more husband to her than the pomegranate seeds that got her into this mess. She was young and naïve, and you could have forgiven her that one mistake rather than dooming us both to this miserable half-life."

As she saw her brother's face harden Demi knew that her anger had once again put her in a precarious position, and Zee's gritted response confirmed it.

"That 'cadaver' is also your brother, madam, in case you've forgotten, with his own rights and feelings. And Persephone may have been young and naïve, but you were not. He asked for her hand properly, offering her the kind of life most young girls long for, and you refused him with no thought for the consequences."

Demi pouted. "She was mine! She's all I had or am likely to have, what with all this work keeping me too busy to cultivate a proper relationship." Her fists clenched as she got back into her stride. "And that's still no excuse for kidnapping her! That's all you boys ever do when you can't get your way, either kidnap the poor things or pretend to be something you're not in order to seduce them. It seems to make no difference that you're already married. It's no wonder you aren't popular with religious types anymore!"

Zee paused to take in this tirade and gazed at his sister thoughtfully. "You may be right that we take too many liberties for our pleasure, and I'm certain my wife would agree. But you and I both know you are throwing stones from a glass house, dear sister. After all, was not Seph's real father married to someone else? In fact, he was married to someone you claim to love. And if that little secret ever came out, what chance would you and your daughter have against the dreaded revenge of your niece, one of the most powerful members in our family?"

"Oh for the gods' sake, it was one night! And we'd had too much ambrosia! Hephaestus doesn't mean anything to me, and Aphro would have understood! It's not like she wasn't already having it off with Ares!"

Zee chuckled nastily. "A fine, logical argument, and one that Aphrodite would have paid no attention to as well you know. The girl isn't blessed with Athena's cool head, more's the pity. Particularly where love is concerned. She wants what's hers, and what belongs to others as well. But this is getting us nowhere. What's done is done, and we still have to deal with the fallout from your ill-conceived action."

Demi lifted her chin in defiance. "It would have happened eventually, you know, even without my intervention. The stuff was just lying down there, waiting to be discovered, thanks to someone throwing a meteor that killed all those lizardy things. Now I wonder who did that?"

"They may or may not have discovered the oil given time," Zee replied, "but you precipitated the current situation by poking a hole in that Pennsylvania field right when the Drake fellow was riding by and couldn't miss it shooting into the air. And I'll have you know the meteor was nothing to do with me. In fact, I don't think it was any of ours. More likely Jehovah or Shiva, one of those fellows always threatening fire and brimstone. Are you forgetting when Jehovah flooded the entire planet just because he wasn't getting enough worship? Talk about a narcissist. We lost a lot of followers thanks to him and his flashy floods."

They both paused in a rare moment of agreement, thinking about how annoying other deities were.

"So," Zee slapped his thighs, causing the house to rumble on its foundations, "what are we going to do about the fact that our favorite planet is about to be decimated yet again? Because this time, it's us who will take the blame, and I don't want to be on the wrong side of that new Flying Spaghetti Monster guy, he's a disaster waiting to happen with all those tentacles. Mind you, Phobo and Apophis would thank us, they're always happy with a bit of fear and chaos. But I'd rather not risk it. You have any ideas?"

"Why do I always have to be one with the ideas?" Demi whined. "I've done everything so far. That American vice president, the one who 'invented' the internet, I spent so much time inspiring him that people eventually started thinking he was obsessed. And if you want to talk about an investment of time, I'm still having to appear in dreams to the Attenborough guy to get him to spread the word about the environment."

"But neither of them have managed to make enough of a difference, have they?" Zee gently replied. "We need something different, something they can't ignore."

"Which is why I went with the little girl last time!" Demi protested. "I mean, who can ignore a really cute, smart little Swedish girl?'"

Zee looked at his sister with pity. "Come on, Demi, not your most brilliant idea, you must admit. People have been ignoring smart little girls since time began. If you wanted to go female, you'd have been better off working with one of those gun-toting southern U.S. politicians, they seem to find a way to make themselves heard."

Demi barked out a laugh. "Please, even I can only do so much. Besides, I think Apophis got to them already, you know how susceptible the ladies are to his snake form."

"Well, we have to do something. People are suffering, and now our least-favourite oligarch is using the situation to withhold oil from the rest of the world."

"But surely that's a good thing? Now they'll have to find alternate energy sources, and our problem will be solved!" Demi sat up hopefully.

Zee shook his head, his crown catching the light and sending sparks around the room. A nearby chair burst into flame, and Demi yelled for a servant to bring some water and put it out before returning her attention to her brother.

"They're all too dependent on it still," he said. "Most of the world has come together to protect things like freedom and justice, which I must say surprised me no little bit, but as soon as they must do without their precious fossil fuel it will be back to me-first politics, and those annoying despots will soon be back on top. I mean, it's one thing for you to get all grumpy when Seph leaves and torture the planet with cold and ice. At least you have something resembling an excuse. But those guys? It's all painful poisons and blowing up civilians, just to keep themselves in yachts and mansions," he finished, glancing around his sister's grandiose palace.

Demi slumped back down. "I just don't know what else I can do. I am sorry for starting all this, but I don't think I can stop it alone. As I said, I have tried."

Zee smiled at her. "I know, Demeter, and that's why I've come to talk to you today. Have your servants bring us some ambrosia and we'll discuss some options I've got in mind."

"Ambrosia? Are you insane? Didn't we just discuss the trouble that follows that stuff? Oh no, I'll have Ganymede bring us a nice tisane, that way no one gets amorous."

Zeus waved his hand in the air, dislodging a lightning bolt which crashed through one of the windows. He was not the easiest house guest.

"Whatever. I think our best bet is in California..."

Dave walked through the front door of Bay Area Labs with a smile on his face and a spring in his step, managing to look almost dapper in his blue jeans, carefully pressed white dress shirt, and black windbreaker. He tossed a bubbling "Cheerio!" at the receptionist and swiped his way through several security doors to reach the fusion lab.

As he hung up his jacket, he noticed his co-worker Phil was already there studying the results from their test the week before. The latter looked up in surprise when Dave settled next to him and slapped him on the back in what could only be described as pure bonhomie. This was very un-Dave-like behavior before noon on a Monday, even considering the success of their recent scientific breakthrough.

"Aren't we a bundle of joy today," Phil remarked with a certain lack of his own luster. He'd had a very early morning dealing with a teething toddler, and Dave's slap had exacerbated an already pounding headache.

"Phil, ol' buddy, I've just had the weekend to end all weekends, and my happiness knows no bounds. I would share the details of said weekend, but a gentleman doesn't tell. Let's just say that a certain redheaded scientist has discovered there's fun to be had at Daveyland."

Dave performed a Pythonesque say-no-more wink that brought Phil right to the edge of regurgitation, but he managed to hold everything in.

"So, Maddie finally agreed to a date, eh? Congratulations. I thought you'd given up after her fourteenth refusal. I'll give you credit for persistence."

"Not only did she agree, but she had such a good time on Saturday night that we ran the date over to Sunday. I'm telling you, pal, this is it. This is the one. She's beautiful, smart, funny and, well, fairly limber, if you know what I mean." Another wink.

"Please," Phil begged, "I'd like to retain the tiny bit of breakfast I managed to shovel in this morning." He covered his face with his hands to still the throbbing of his head. Young love was so not what he needed today. Young love led to marriage, which often led to children, which led to teething. He managed to brighten a bit at the thought of Dave suffering these torments in the future.

Dave attempted a sympathetic demeanor but couldn't help that his eyes continued to twinkle with excitement. "Aw, man, kid keeping you up again?"

Phil simply nodded in misery.

"Poor sop. Anything I can do? I'm headed to the kitchen; can I get you a hit of java?"

Phil gestured to his nearly empty recycle cup with gratitude.

Anything to get a few more minutes of peace away from Mr. Just-Got-Laid. As Dave grabbed the cup and bounced to the kitchen, Phil thought back to when he and his wife had started dating. They'd had so much energy, they couldn't keep their hands off each other. It had been an incredibly happy time, enough to carry them through the challenges that followed, including their current sleep-deprived existence. It really wasn't fair of him, he decided, to rain on his lab partner's parade.

When Dave returned with the coffee, Phil popped a couple more aspirin from the bottle near his elbow and turned to his friend with a determined smile.

"I'm really glad for ya, buddy. I know you've been hoping she'd say yes for a while. And I'm totally unsurprised that she's discovered what a great guy she's been missing. I have to tell you right now, though, that I do not want to hear details. I have to continue to work with Maddie, so it's best if I don't know what tattoo she has where in case I let something slip or get distracted. Capeesh?"

Dave smiled and nodded happily. "Of course. Sordid details are what high school buddies are for, eh? Now, what are your thoughts on our next steps with the lasers? I don't want to be presumptuous, but I have some ideas for speeding up the path to commercialization."

Phil looked at his partner with eyebrows raised. "You had time for that?" he joked. "Well, good. It always tees me off a bit that after you spend over a decade working on getting a decent fusion reaction to release excess energy, all the government types immediately want to know is when you'll be saving the world. A world that is mostly in the mess it's in because those same government types are too cowardly to save it themselves."

Phil noticed his head was pounding again as Dave let out a quick bark of laughter.

"Dude, dial down the politics, eh? I'm sorry your world is so gloomy, but in mine the sun is definitely high in the sky, the flowers are blooming, and the little birdies are all tweeting a tune. Which, by the way, isn't far off reality on this fine spring day. Maybe you need to go take a walk outside, inhale some nice clean fresh air?"

Phil sighed. "You're probably right. Sorry to be such a grouch. Give me a few minutes and I'll be back so we can discuss your ideas." He rose and left the room, a bemused Dave looking after him fondly.

Outside it was as Dave described. The sun was gently warming, and there were daffodils blooming along both sides of the path, their heads graciously waving in the soft April breeze. Spring was such a beautiful time in northern California. Phil could feel his headache ease as Pat Boone's crooning version of *April Love* hummed through it. His wife loved that old movie, and Phil decided he'd order the DVD as a gift. They could watch it together the next time little Bryan slept. If he ever slept.

A familiar white Subaru pulled into a parking space on his left. After a minute, the redheaded topic of this morning's conversation stepped out of it.

Maddie Bingham was indeed a looker. Even in khaki trousers and an overstretched pink sweater her beauty shone through. Phil knew from working with the woman over the past year that Dave was also right about her being an excellent scientist.

But that was where his friend's accuracy stopped, because the woman before him was not happy. Where, Phil thought, was the *joie de vivre* to match Dave's? Shouldn't there at least be a quiet satisfaction at a weekend pleasantly spent discovering a new romance? This was not the face of love's young dream. Maddie's frown didn't budge as she tersely nodded at Phil on her way past him into the building.

In the sky, the sun drifted behind a cloud that Phil could swear hadn't been there a moment before, and he felt a sudden chill. Time to head back inside.

He was a few paces from the door to the fusion lab when he heard voices. Obviously, Maddie had gotten there before him. Not wanting to interrupt their reunion, Phil dawdled outside the door, somewhat unashamedly eavesdropping.

"But ... w-what are you talking about?" Phil heard his lab partner stutter. "You know we had a great time this weekend. You said so yourself just yesterday. What's going on?"

Maddie's voice was quieter. Phil had to practically put his ear to the door to hear her.

"I'm sorry, Dave, but I guess I was just caught up in the idea of it all. After some thought yesterday, I know I'm not ready to get involved in a new relationship so soon after my last one. And even if I was, I'm not sure you would be the right choice. You don't want to be rebound guy, do you?"

"Oh, Maddie." Phil could hear the despair in Dave's voice. "I want to be the guy who gets to be near you. Labels don't matter. You can't deny we were good together. You can't just throw all that away. Please reconsider. Maybe try one more date to see how things go?"

Phil could imagine Maddie shaking her head. "It won't do any good. I'm decided on this. It was a lovely weekend, Dave, but I just don't see that we have a future together, and I don't want to lead you on."

Phil barely had time to take a few steps away from the door and turn as if he was coming in before Maddie came striding through it. She passed him without acknowledgement, and Phil looked through the door's circular window to see his friend crushed with sorrow, his head and hands hanging limply in front of him.

Phil entered the room and patted his partner on the back in a depressing echo of Dave's recent joyous slap.

"I'm so sorry, Dave. Truly. We've all been there, and I know how it hurts."

Dave just shook his head back and forth, tears starting to run down his cheeks and plop onto the immaculately clean linoleum floor.

"I don't understand," he moaned. "Everything was so right. I swear to you, she was having as good a time as I was, I just don't get what went wrong."

Phil put an arm around his dejected friend and gave him a slight squeeze. It was as much as manliness allowed.

"Well, I think you've just learned the hard way that women are a mystery. They just don't think the way we do. Maybe we should have been working on solving that mystery instead of creating a viable new form of energy."

Dave rose from his chair and shuffled over to the coat rack where he retrieved his jacket.

"I'm going home," he muttered over his shoulder on his way out the door. "I'm just too damn depressed to work right now."

Phil watched him leave with growing sympathy. Poor guy. If he was telling the truth about their weekend, what a crushing blow it must be for Maddie to have reversed course so completely. He'd give Dave a couple of days and then call and check up on him, maybe beg his wife for some time off to take his friend out to cheer him up.

But a couple of days later, Phil was surprised when he called Dave and found his number was disconnected. And he was even more surprised when their manager told him a few days later that Dave had quit for "personal reasons". He'd never been to Dave's house, had no idea where he lived, so that was that.

The knock on Demi's door was even more thunderous this time, if that was possible. It put her in an instant bad mood since Seph was sleeping upstairs and she'd promised her daughter a luxurious lie-in. It was such a delight having her home again, and Demi resented any intrusion on their happiness.

She opened the door and Zee pounded his way in, cracking the marble floor with the force of his footsteps. Behind him sauntered her niece Aphrodite, chin held high and looking her usual stunningly gorgeous self. Without asking, they both headed into the parlor and took seats at the opposite sides of the room. Demi noticed Zee was facing away from her recently repaired window, which at least lessened the chance it would get broken again. She sat by the doorway, equidistant from them both, and gave them each a questioning look.

"It's all ruined," Zeus stated, glaring at the goddess of love.

Aphrodite gazed past him out the window with calculated boredom.

"What, pray tell, is ruined?" said Demeter.

"Everything." Zee turned to face his sister. "You remember the scientist in California? The one I told you was our best hope of saving the planet?"

Demi nodded. "Of course. Have you forgotten how much time I spent helping him get his life in order so he could do the necessary work? I even had to barter favors with the Muses to get them to provide inspiration for his love life as well as his profession, and those ladies drive a hard bargain. I will owe them for years."

"Then I'm sure you'll understand my ... annoyance ... when I tell you that's all been for nothing." Zeus threw another furious glance at his daughter, who was still intent on ignoring him.

Demi began to suspect Aphrodite had once again done something atrocious.

"What's happened?" she asked her brother, marveling at how so much beauty could cause so many problems. She remembered the Trojan War as if it was yesterday, all that mud and those dead bodies mucking up her beloved fields.

"Do you want to tell her, or should I?" Zeus asked his daughter. Aphrodite finally deigned to look at her father but remained silent.

"Fine." He turned to Demeter. "Your niece sent her son to shoot Maddie Bingham with a love arrow."

Demi felt like she'd lost the plot. "Maddie? The object of affection for our scientist?"

Zee nodded.

"But that's fine, right? I mean, the last time I checked, they were having a glorious weekend together. Does it matter if it's because of our arrangements, or due to one of Cupid's arrows? Surely the result is the same?"

Zee sighed. "You don't understand. She ordered Cupid to shoot the woman *after* her weekend with Dave, after she'd left his house. Maddie was doomed to fall madly in love with the next person she saw.

Which in this case, was the bag girl at the grocery store she visited on her way home."

Demi's jaw hung open in shock. "So, Dave is...?"

"In Tibet, studying to become a monk. He's taken it very badly. Given up his career before he could share any of the ideas we implanted. Best scenario, the project is set back twenty years, which will, of course, be too late."

"Couldn't we start over, inspire another scientist?" Demi wanted to know.

Zee stamped his foot in exasperation and a lightning bolt slipped out of the belt on his back, its edge catching the window. Demi sighed as the glass shattered. Again.

"There isn't time!" Zee thundered. "No one left has the proper background, and it would take decades to raise someone from scratch. No, this has done for that poor planet, and the human race has your niece to thank for its extermination."

Demi looked at Aphrodite, now gloriously stretched out on the sofa. "Why?" Demi asked her. "Why did you do this?"

Her question finally elicited a response from the goddess, who sat up and glowered at her aunt.

"You have the GALL to ask me that?" she snarled. "This is YOUR fault, and I refuse to take the blame!"

Demi recoiled from the hatred in her niece's tone, her temper as passionate as her capacity for love.

"What on earth are you talking about? How can this be my fault? I didn't force you to ruin the one decent chance the earth had of surviving!"

Aphrodite visibly forced herself to relax, but anger still simmered in her violet eyes as she quirked a perfectly shaped eyebrow at her aunt.

"Didn't you?" she purred. "How did you expect me to respond after discovering you seduced my HUSBAND and bore him that bitch daughter?"

Demeter had lost the power of speech. Looking over at Zeus, she could tell he'd known the secret was out before bringing Aphrodite to her door. The father of the gods was sending her a look that distinctly declared "I told you so". Pulling herself together, Demi addressed her niece as calmly as she could, hoping rationality might defuse the situation.

"Aphrodite, I had no plans to seduce Hephaestus." (An unladylike snort from the goddess of love.) "There was ambrosia, and I was crazed with mourning the departure of Persephone, who by the way has no idea who her father is and is innocent in all this. I am very sorry if I hurt you, it was never my intention and, except for the joy of having my daughter, I honestly wish it hadn't happened. Please forgive me. It's not like Heph threw you over for me, he's never been less than madly in love with you."

She saw Aphrodite soften at her words, so she went on.

"Besides, it's not like you've never seduced someone's husband, so maybe you can give me a little bit of slack on this, particularly as it happened so very long ago?"

Demi instantly realized she should have quit while she was ahead. Aphrodite jumped to her feet, eyes blazing. "I am the goddess of love! It is my duty to spread love everywhere I go! I suggest in future you stick to the things you do best, growing your weeds half the year and punishing your beloved humans the other half simply because you didn't get your way with Hades!" Her niece stomped out of the house in a huff of rose-scented rage.

After a moment, Demi turned her attention back to Zeus. "Is there nothing more we can do for the humans, Zee?" she asked. She'd never seen her brother look quite so dejected.

"Not from a positive point of view," he replied. "I've taken it to the council of the gods. Jehovah has, of course, suggested another flood, but we all agree that's a last resort. There are a lot more large boats around this time, and we'd have no control over who got saved. We may have to go with Wen Shen's idea of a pandemic, at least that will leave the youngest for us to build a new world with."

They both sat in silence, saddened by the fate of such a once-promising planet.

"Well," said Demeter, "for whatever it's worth, I'm going to give them the most glorious spring they've ever seen. What with global warming, I should be able to create some magnificent new tropical zones for them to enjoy, and all kinds of juicy fruits to eat before the ice caps melt and they drown."

Zeus moved to sit next to his sister and took her hand gently in his. "You are, as ever, a gracious goddess, sister."

Demi suddenly had a thought. "How did Aphro find out about my affair with Heph?"

Zeus sat back and laughed. "It was your young servant Ganymede. Seems he was her spy, placed in your household to keep her up to date on any gossip."

Demeter frowned. "The one you stole? That little imp! I should have known he was one of hers, he was entirely too helpful. Have you had a talk with him?"

Zeus looked extremely self-satisfied. "We have ... talked ... and he now knows where his loyalties lie. He is proving to be an excellent cup bearer."

Demeter rolled her eyes. Planets may come and go, but her brother never changed.

Gianetta Murray

Gianetta is a retired technical writer and librarian. She grew up in Silicon Valley, where she wrote everything from technical specifications to website, marketing, and newspaper copy. She was a Toastmasters county champion in Storytelling, and she won a Daniel Phelan writing award for a short story casting Peter Rabbit as St. Augustine. She moved to Yorkshire, England almost 20 years ago when she married a Brit, and she is working on getting her first cozy mystery novel published.

gianettamurray.com

Nante

By Eden Monroe

NANTE CAME INTO MY LIFE early one spring, or at least I think he did.

I'll never forget it. I'd just settled in at the library, a landmark in our small town, trying to concentrate on the page in front of me. I was supposed to be studying for a psychology exam, but the balmy night outside beckoned, the tiny spring peeper frogs pinging their age-old serenade in the lake not far away.

Lost in thought, I jumped when a man spoke to me. "Did you think I wouldn't look for you in the library, Rosalie?" he asked in contravention of Maybelline Holt's out-dated rule of silence.

I gaped at him. "Excuse me?" I asked, dumbfounded, and was enthusiastically shushed by Miss Holt.

He laughed quietly, and I appreciated the deep throaty sound. "Come now, let's not play games. We had a disagreement, but it's over, now let's go home and make up properly."

"Do I know you?" I whispered, staring at the handsome stranger.

"R-o-s-a-l-i-e," he said, drawing my name out reprovingly.

"I'm sorry," I said, shaking my head, "I *am* Rosalie, but I have no idea who you are."

Tap tap tap tap went Miss Holt's sturdy oxfords, rapping out a no-nonsense staccato as she marched into battle on the polished hardwood floor. Her pursed lips meant certain eviction, and I saw my study time going out the window.

"Please be quiet! If you two want to have a conversation, I suggest you leave," she reprimanded in undertones.

"I don't want to have a conversation with this man," I told her.

"Tell *him* to leave."

"I want you both to leave. If you and Nante have had a quarrel, you can settle it elsewhere."

"But..." I persisted.

"Rosalie...." Maybelline Holt warned.

Seething, I slammed my textbook shut and headed for the door, Nante hot on my heels.

"Rosalie, please,"he called after me as we made our way outside, "don't waste such a beautiful spring evening being angry."

I turned to face him at the bottom of the worn granite steps and had to admit he looked mighty good under the dusk-to-dawn light at the corner of the building. His hair was black, slightly overlong with soft waves that framed his face to perfection. His nose was straight and aristocratic, his mouth sensual, teasing.

He wore a rumpled white tuxedo shirt with just enough buttons open to reveal a tantalizing glimpse of a silver medallion on a chain. A black blazer, jeans and scuffed cowboy boots clearly said I'm sexy, but I don't care.

"Look," I said, "I don't know you! I've never laid eyes on you before tonight. As much as I'd like to be who you think I am ... Monty ... I'm not."

He laughed again, indulgently. "You must stop this charade, Sugar. I know you know my name; it's still ringing in my ears from last night. Over and over again. Nante! Oh, Nante!"

I could feel my face burn. "I beg your pardon," I said slowly. "I repeat, I have never seen you before. I don't know you, and quite frankly you're way over the line. This conversation is finished."

"Rosalie, sweetheart..." His brow knit in a puzzled frown. "I don't know what's come over you."

I tucked my book under my arm and turned to leave, hoping he would take the hint. I'd only gone a few steps when for the second time that night a voice from behind startled me.

"Rosalie! Nante! Hello! Nice to see you two!" said my friend,

Theresa, as she hurried up to where I was standing. "Just want to say again how much fun we had on Saturday night. We have to get together again soon. We could have a barbecue at our place, and Nante," she said, turning her attention to him, "make sure to bring your guitar. Everybody is still talking about how well you two sing together." She checked her watch. "Ooops! Gotta run. I have to pick Sylvie up from ballet practice. Ciao!" And with that she continued on down the street, her shoulder-length ponytail swaying as she trotted away.

Nante was looking at me with a definite *I told you so* expression, one eyebrow raised quizzically, waiting for my reaction.

I felt totally at sea. It also occurred to me that maybe I was losing my mind. It was beginning to feel like a distinct possibility.

"We really do sing well together, Sugar." He smiled again disarmingly.

"Sugar?" I asked in exasperation.

"That's my pet name for you."

"Great!"

A smile slid slowly across his face. "That's because you're so sweet, but let's also say I think you're pretty hot stuff."

I tried to ignore that, but with difficulty. "Oh really, and what's my pet name for you?"

He threw back his head and laughed. "Mostly you just call me babe, but I love it."

I stared at him again. Babe was what I used to call my ex-fiancé, Nick, so it wasn't a pet name I'd never used before.

"Look ... uh, Mon ..." I began.

"Nante," he corrected, his eyes twinkling.

"Nante. I'm sure you're a very nice man, but this is all a little too crazy, even for me. I've been accused of having a vivid imagination, but this goes way beyond that. Maybe this is just a dream. Maybe I'm in some weird time warp, but I've never..."

"I know, seen me before in your life. Rosalie, maybe you should see a doctor. It could be some kind of amnesia. Did you bump your head?"

I shook my head. "No, I didn't bump ... anything and I don't have amnesia!"

Nante stepped forward and gently laid his hands on my shoulders. "I don't know sweetheart, but something is definitely wrong. All I can tell you is that we're in love, have been since we met really. You like to tell everyone it was love at first sight. I know it was that for me. Come on, I'll walk you home. Maybe after a good night's sleep you'll feel better."

As we started away he dropped an arm around my shoulders, and curiously enough it felt right.

The red light was blinking on my answering machine when I got to my apartment. It was my mother.

"I just wanted to invite you and Nante over to supper tomorrow evening. I'm cooking your favorite, so give me a call when you come in and let me know if you can make it." Beep.

I slowly settled onto the edge of the small striped chair beside the telephone table. So my mother knows Nante too. In fact, everybody seemed to know him, except me. I quickly dialed my mother's number and was relieved when she answered instead of having to leave a message.

"I got your invitation," I said. "Or I should say *we* did."

Pleasure was evident in my mother's voice. "Good."

"Sooo, you like Nante do you?"

There was a brief silence. "Well of course I do, darling, we all do. Haven't I told you that on several occasions? Nante is a wonderful man, and you're fortunate to have met him."

I cleared my throat. "How long have we ... er ... been going out?"

"I don't know, six months or so. Why?"

"Do you happen to remember how we met?" I asked, trying to sound nonchalant.

"At the library as I recall, something about you studying for one of your psychology exams. Yes, it was definitely at the library."

I felt the hair on the back of my neck begin to rise. "Hmmm... Right. Are we in love?"

I hadn't meant to ask that last question, it just sort of slipped out.

Now my mother sounded concerned, you could hear it. "I expect so, you both certainly act as though you are. Are you all right, Rosalie? That's a peculiar question."

"Yes. I mean I'm all right. Just doing a little soul searching is all."

"All right then, we'll see you both for dinner tomorrow night, and bring your appetite."

I smiled at the familiar tag line. "Sure, see you then."

We rang off and I glanced over at my psychology book lying on the sofa. I was considering a different career path, taking evening classes to boost my credits. That exam was scheduled for next week, however tonight was the first time I had ever gone to the library to study.

The phone rang, jarring me from my thoughts.

"Are you feeling better now, Rosalie?" came the low sultry tone that I recognized immediately as Nante.

"Ye-yes, I'm fine," I lied for the second time in less than five minutes.

"You're sure?" he pressed.

"Everything's fine. I'm just tired I guess," and more than a little confused I wanted to add.

"You have me worried, Sugar. Get some sleep and I'm sure tomorrow will be a better day. I love you," and with the sound of a kiss he said goodnight.

Sugar wasn't sure if she could sleep or not, but after a cup of herbal tea I slipped between the sheets. Analyze. Predicament: I have a drop-dead gorgeous guy who's in love with me, only I've never met him before. Problem: Everyone else seems to know him except me but if I had amnesia, I wouldn't remember anything or anyone would I?

It was only Nante that I appeared to have forgotten. Everything else seemed to be intact. Maybe there was such a thing as romantic amnesia, but why wouldn't it kick in and erase some of the miserable dates I'd had in the past? Someone like Nante comes along and boom! I forget him.

About 2:00 a.m. I came to the conclusion that I'd just play along with the Nante thing. What did I have to lose? If he was in love with me, maybe I could come to love him too. From what I'd seen so far, that shouldn't be too difficult. He certainly seemed worth the try, and besides, everyone else thought he was a great guy. Maybe I would too. Only a fool would pinch themselves to wake up from *him*.

Not surprisingly I was soon head over heels in love with Nante. Amnesia or whatever, it was most certainly a blessing. The past two and a half months had been idyllic, and I kept putting off telling him I was pregnant, not wanting to say anything until I was reasonably certain. One evening as I lay cradled in his arms, I knew the moment of truth was at hand.

"Nante, I have something to tell you," I began hesitantly.

"What, that you're pregnant?" I could hear the smile in his voice.

I raised up quickly on one elbow to look at him. "You know?"

"Sugar," he said gently as though scolding a child, "don't you think I know every inch of the woman I love? Do you really think I wouldn't notice that you're carrying my child?"

Try as I might, I couldn't seem to stem the flow of tears.

"Those are tears of joy I hope," he said stroking my hair. "You do want this baby, don't you?"

I sniffed. "Of course I do. I love you, Nante. How could I not love our baby?"

"Then all is well. We'll have a happy future together, you and I and our little one. Have you been to see a doctor?"

"Ummm, no," I admitted.

"Rosalie! Make an appointment tomorrow. I want you and the

baby to be healthy." He shifted onto his side to face me, brushing the last of my tears away with the pad of his thumb. "You look beautiful. Your tears make your face shine."

My doctor examined me two days later and announced that I did indeed appear to be pregnant, but lab tests were necessary to confirm it. He also felt I was further along than I'd imagined, but then again, my jeans *were* starting to get a little tight.

"But it's only been a couple of months," I told him, bewildered.

He smiled. "Well, I'm guessing you're into your second trimester, Rosalie."

There was a cancellation that afternoon for an ultrasound, so I was booked in, stopping in at the clinic along the way for blood tests.

I got to the Imaging Department with minutes to spare, excited as I waited for the procedure to begin. I would have loved to have Nante there with me, but he couldn't get away from the office.

The ultrasonographer positioned the screen so that I could watch. On went the ice-cold jelly as the transducer was guided over my abdomen with practiced hands. She smiled but remained silent, intent at her task as she studied the monitor, seemingly perplexed.

"Please excuse me for a moment," she said setting down the instrument and pulling the sheet back into place. "I'll be right back."

True to her word she quickly returned with a colleague.

"What is it? What's wrong?" I demanded, pushing myself into a sitting position.

"Please try to relax, Rosalie. We're just having a bit of trouble with the image," I was reassured, but I didn't miss the look that passed between them.

Five more minutes and it was finally over. I was advised that my doctor would be in touch.

Dr. Sherwood's office called the next day and it seemed like forever until I was ushered into his office.

"Have a seat, Rosalie," the doctor said from behind his desk after I'd closed the door after me.

"What's wrong with my baby?" I asked him, still standing.

"Please ... sit down," was all he said, indicating the empty chair opposite his desk.

I sat down stiffly on the edge of the seat. "You have bad news, I can tell."

He cleared his throat uncomfortably. "There's no easy way to tell you this, my dear, but you're not pregnant. The ultrasound could not detect the presence of a fetus, and the blood tests were negative."

A curious weakness flooded through me. "But you examined me and said I was pregnant!"

"I did a preliminary exam, and you did appear to be pregnant, but there is no baby in your womb."

"What do you mean, there is no baby!" I demanded, nausea curling in my stomach. "I have all the symptoms! All of them! How could there be no baby?"

He straightened in his chair. "You really wanted a baby didn't you, Rosalie?"

"Don't try to psychoanalyze me, please," I said, choking back tears. "I got pregnant ... I am pregnant! I repeat, how could there be no baby? There's something wrong with the ultrasound, there has to be."

"I believe you have what's called pseudocyesis, a pseudo pregnancy, or a false pregnancy. Oh you'll have all the signs and symptoms. Your belly will enlarge, but in truth you only imagined you were pregnant. It's unfortunate, and I'm very sorry to give you this news. This is very difficult, but it's not the end of everything. You can still get pregnant. Next time it will probably be the real thing."

"Probably!" I cried, still reeling.

"Nature can be peculiar sometimes, and there's no explaining why certain things happen. Now that we know the truth, your symptoms in all likelihood will disappear. You should very quickly return to normal."

"*Again,* maybe it's the ultrasound that's wrong," I argued stubbornly. "Machines do make mistakes."

Sighing, Dr. Sherwood leaned forward, his elbows resting on the desk in front of him. "Your womb is empty, Rosalie. It was quite clear on the ultrasound image. There is no baby, and again, the lab tests were negative. You are definitely not pregnant. I'm sorry. Now I apologize but I have other patients I must see. Feel free to take a few minutes to collect yourself before you leave."

Back home in my apartment I let my supervisor know I didn't feel well and wouldn't be in for the rest of the day. Then I called Nante's cell. My call was answered quickly but it was a frail voice on the other end of the line.

"Is Nante there?" I asked, willing the impatience from my voice.

"Who?" came the feeble question.

"Is Nante there?" I repeated, trying to be a little less demanding.

"I'm sorry, dear, there is no one here by that name,"

"Oh, I must have called the wrong number."

I dialed again, carefully, but it was the same elderly woman who answered.

Frustrated, I apologized once more and hung up. What was going on! Where was Nante?

It was nearly noon and I knew my mother would be taking a break from her writing.

"Hi, Mum, is Nante there?" I asked without preamble after her cheerful hello.

There was a frightening hesitation. "Who is Nante?"

"Who is Nante! My boyfriend, Nante, the same one who was there last Saturday painting your fence. You know, dark hair, good looking. I thought maybe he went over there for lunch."

I tried to inject some levity, but it failed as the bubble of panic rose painfully in my chest once again,

"What is going on, Rosalie? I've never heard of anyone by that name, and it was *you* who painted my fence, dear. Is this some kind of joke?"

"I'll ask you the same question, Mum. One minute Nante is the best thing that ever happened to me, and the next you don't know who he is ... and I did *not* paint your fence. Nante did! He also cleaned out your tulip bed. How could you forget?"

And with that I hung up. I'd call her later when I got this whole thing straightened out.

Next I dialed Nante's workplace. His cell obviously wasn't working but he'd be in his office. Stephanie, the over-the-top receptionist, announced the name of the company with her usual gusto. A friendly person, the two of us had shared a lengthy conversation at the recent company dinner.

"Hi, Stephanie," I said. "This is Rosalie, is Nante there?"

There was a pause. "I'm sorry, who are you looking for?" she asked in a professionally distant voice.

"This is Rosalie. You remember, from the dinner two weeks ago? I'm Nante's girlfriend. I was just wondering if he was there or has he left for lunch?" He was probably on his way over to my place even as we spoke.

"I'm sorry, Rosemary, but I think you have the wrong number. There is no one here by that name. Do you have the correct company I wonder?"

"I have the right company. My name is Rosalie, not Rosemary. Rosalie Turner. You and I met when I accompanied Nante to the company dinner. Don't you remember? We talked about your dog, Max."

"No, Ma'm, I think you have mistaken me for somebody else. I don't have a dog and we don't have anybody here by the name of Rontay or whatever."

"Nante is his name, Nante Pineo. He is your graphic designer."

"I've been with Foster & Wills for almost ten years and we've *never* had anyone here by that name. Our graphic designer is Tom Stilwell. Would you like to speak to our manager?"

I resisted the urge to throw the phone … throw something! Instead, I slammed the receiver down with uncharacteristic rudeness and immediately regretted doing so.

Visibly shaking I called my friend Theresa. She didn't take her lunch hour until one o'clock so she should still be at her desk. One ring, two rings, three rings. Finally, she answered.

By this point I was in tears and struggled to find my voice. "Theresa," I managed.

"Rosalie? What's the matter, are you all right?"

I took a deep breath, "I'm all right, just not having such a great day you could say. Listen, have you seen Nante? I know he was supposed to get together with Bill, and I thought maybe you might know when that is."

The now all too familiar hesitation followed. "What are you talking about, Rosalie? Who's Nante?"

"Nante, my boyfriend."

"I didn't know you had a boyfriend. Aren't you the sly one. Tell me about him."

My knuckles were white as I tightened my grip on the receiver. "I suppose you're going to tell me you've never met him either."

"Rosalie, I have never met anybody named Nante. Is that a nickname or something?"

"No, that's his name. He plays the guitar, remember? We were over to your place just a week ago, and you guys have been here. Come on!"

"I'm kind of busy, hon. I can tell you're upset, but I honestly don't know anybody by that name. The last I heard you were dating Nick somebody or other. Let's get together soon for coffee and you can tell me about your new fella."

My heart felt as though it was going to leap out of my chest, but I remained calm with an effort. "Sure. I'll give you a call."

I slowly replaced the receiver. Was Nante just a figment of my imagination? No! Suddenly I remembered the photo of him that I carried in my purse, but a thorough search for it proved to be in vain.

Oh! Maybelline Holt, the town's fastidious librarian. Of course! She would remember Nante. She had thrown us out of the library, surely she couldn't have forgotten that.

But Nante? Miss Holt had no such recollection of that night ... or Nante ... when I reached her at the library.

Later as I lay in bed, my pillow drenched with tears, I placed a hand on my empty womb. There never was a baby, there never was a Nante. Midnight came and went, and still no sleep. Clawing back the covers, I made my way to the bathroom cabinet and found the sleeping pills I'd been prescribed for insomnia a few months ago ... before Nante.

Sleep claimed me surprisingly quickly, and for the next eight hours I was stalked and tortured by nightmares. At last Nante came to me and I sank weakly into his arms.

"You frightened me," I wept. "I thought I had only imagined you, everyone did. But you're here now; we're together again."

He hugged me tightly. "There, there, Sugar. Everything's going to be all right. Because you need me, I'm here, and I am very real. How could you doubt my love for you?" He tenderly pulled a shawl around my shoulders to stop my shivering.

I felt comforted and secure, although I thought to tease him that he had wrapped me up a little too tightly. I tried to loosen the shawl, but I couldn't, it was wound securely in place, and I could no longer see Nante. Flailing wildly, the cursed shawl held firm.

"Nante! Nante!"

"I'm here, Sugar, not far away. Come to me," but his voice gradually faded into the ether.

Somehow, I got through the next few weeks. I put Nante out of my mind as best I could. I tried to forget about the fake pregnancy and got on with my life. I was grateful too that the nightmares had all but subsided, however the aching emptiness inside of me that I knew only Nante could fill, remained cold and vacant.

Spring had now blossomed into summer in all its golden glory and one sunny Saturday I decided to go to the beach a short distance from where my mother lived. I left my beach stuff at her place rather than carry it back and forth, and Mum told me she'd slipped a new novel into my blue canvas bag to read while I sunbathed. Mum and I often exchanged books, and she promised that I'd *really* enjoy this one.

The sky was cloudless as I spread out the blanket, put the pillow in place and settled down for a good read.

As was my habit I skipped the back cover blurb and got right into the novel, my eyes widening as I began to read:

Nante came into my life early one spring, or at least I think he did.

I'll never forget it. I'd just settled in at the library, a landmark in our small town, trying to concentrate on the page in front of me. I was supposed to be studying for a psychology exam, but the balmy night outside beckoned, tiny spring peeper frogs pinging their age-old serenade in the lake not far away.

Lost in thought, I jumped when a man spoke to me. "Did you think I wouldn't look for you in the library, Rosalie?" he asked in contravention of Maybelline Holt's out-dated rule of silence.

I gaped at him. "Excuse me?" I asked, dumbfounded, and was enthusiastically shushed by Miss Holt.

He laughed quietly, and I appreciated the deep throaty sound. "Come now, let's not play games. We had a disagreement, but it's over, now let's go home and make up properly."

"Do I know you?" I whispered, staring at the handsome stranger.

"R-o-s-a-l-i-e," he said, drawing my name out reprovingly.

"I'm sorry," I said, shaking my head, "I am Rosalie, but I have no idea who you are."

I threw down the book as though I'd been burned, then just as quickly retrieved it from where it had landed face down in the sand. I looked at the cover. ALWAYS TOGETHER was the title embossed in raised gold letters, and there beneath the bold inscription was the artist's conception of Nante, myself and an adorable little girl with long auburn curls.

I stared at it in disbelief. That was it. I *was* losing my mind! I dropped the book again, and with elbows on knees covered my face with my hands. "What is happening?" I wailed aloud, but only the pounding surf replied.

Just then I heard voices, far off at first, dancing on the wind in the distance and watched as a man came into view. My God! It was Nante!

My heart shouted his name, but before it could escape my lips, I saw the outline of a tall woman beside him. She turned away and it seemed she was calling someone. Then I saw her, a little girl, running along the edge of the waves, bubbling with childish laughter.

I knew it was Nante who stood there silhouetted against the sparkling ocean. I'd know him anywhere.

I watched as the woman and child joined him, my heart crashing against my ribs, my breath trapped in a painful knot.

"Nante," I breathed, closing my eyes. "Oh my, Nante."

My whole body jolted as though from a surge of electricity. There was an explosion of awareness that sucked the air from my lungs and just as quickly refueled my soul with a starburst of happiness as he called out to me and the child.

He watched with a smile as I scooped her into my arms and walked back to where he stood looking up the beach.

"What is it, Momma?" our little girl asked, turning her attention in the direction of her father's gaze.

"What do you see, Nante?" I asked placing my hand over my eyes to shield them from the sun.

"Just an empty blanket and a pillow on the sand I guess," he shrugged. "Somebody must have left them behind."

As we continued our stroll, I glanced over as the pages of a novel cavorted mischievously in the late-morning breeze.

"They left their book behind too," I said, smiling as I held my husband's hand, "but they'll be back...."

Eden Monroe

Eden Monroe loves giving voice to the endless parade of interesting characters who introduce themselves in her imagination. In her novels she writes about real life, real issues and struggles, and triumphing against all odds. In her short stories she likes to color outside the lines. A proud east coast Canadian, she enjoys a variety of outdoor activities, and a good book.

www.edenmonroeauthor.com

Two Bees Curios & Collectables

By Allan Hudson

"WHERE THE HECK ARE YOU, BOOTS?"

The answer comes from the back room of the shop with the clanging and crashing of falling objects, the smashing of glass.

"Eeeee, I'm ... I'm in here Biscuits. Come get this damn thing off me."

Biscuits drops the box she was carrying and runs to the storage area at the back of the store. She halts at the doorway. Gasps at the mess, hands to her mouth. Debris is spread over the floor; a ceramic cat with no head, a confused pile of pots with their handles pointing the blame at each other, shattered figurines and shards of glass from the vase collection turn the aisle into torture alley. The mess lies next to a plastic and metal storage unit with four shelves. Four feet wide, eighteen inches deep, the top shelf, at sixty-six inches, is the same height as Boots' forehead.

"Oh no, the Lalique vase is broken."

"Never mind the damn vase, Biscuits, get this ... this contraption off. I can hardly keep the weight off my head."

"Yeah, yeah Boots. I have to be careful, there's a lot of glass around you. Oh Damn!"

"What? What, Oh Damn?"

Her long hair is scattered under her head like Medusa's snakes. One white vinyl boot sticks through the second and bottom shelf. A four-quart saucepan is balanced on her exposed midriff between shelves three and two, her pink blouse is bunched up under shelf three. Her face is framed by a brass sandpiper pecking at its pedestal, which looks like it smacked her left cheek before resting on the floor. On the right are shards and chunks of colored glass, the remains of matching ruby wine glasses. A rosy splinter sticks out of her chin. Her arms are bent with the hands pinned by the third shelf.

"Don't move your head Boots, there's glass beside it. Let me get around you. Hang on."

Biscuits bends to grab the shelf straddling Boots and sees the splinter of glass.

"Hold still, you have a piece of glass sticking in your chin, just a sliver."

"I can feel it. It stings. Can you pull it out?"

"Uh-huh."

She smiles down at her friend and gently pulls the glass free. Thankfully it's slim, like a darning needle. She tosses it aside and watches the blood make a red pimple over the wound but doesn't run.

"Okay. It's good. Get ready."

"Oh, I'm more than ready."

Biscuits is a stocky girl, no fat but solid bones, six inches shorter than her friend at five two. They weigh the same. The shelving weighs the same too, so it's a struggle for Biscuits to lift the 125-pound unit. Once it's high enough and Boots can help some with her feet, she gets it back on its base and against the wall. Boots lifts her head reaching for Biscuit's outstretched hand.

"Careful where you move, Boots, lots of glass on your right. Sit up first, then step toward me and to the left when you get up. Can you stand?"

"Yeah, I can with your help. Oh shit, my head hurts."

Biscuits grimaces at the sight of the welt on her friend's forehead and a red mark on her cheek.

"I imagine. You took a whack on the forehead."

"I got my hands on the shelf when it was falling and was able to lessen the blow so it coulda been worse."

Boots is standing clear of the debris shifting her blouse in place.

Before tucking it back in her jeans, she reaches under and straightens her bra replacing one breast which popped out when the shelf pushed her blouse up. She re-arranges the beads around her neck, runs her fingers through her hair and fluffs it. She normally just shakes her head and the long curly strands fall in place and flare out at her shoulder blades. She reaches up to touch her forehead, and yanks her finger away, a sour look on her face.

"Ouch ... that smarts. Oh, darn Biscuits. What does it look like?"

Biscuits holds her hand over her mouth, trying not to snicker.

"It ... it looks like you have a red bandana on, too much blush on one cheek and a red birthmark on your chin."

Boots frowns at her friend who finds it comical, but Biscuit's girlish giggles are infectious and she imagines her red forehead.

"Oh, don't make me laugh, it makes my head hurt."

"I'm sorry Boots, the darndest thing is, it looks good on you. Red is your color."

"Stop. I hope there is aspirin in the first aid kit."

"Yeah. Hey, you're our first casualty. Now aren't you glad I put that kit together. I'll be right back. Meet me at the front counter."

She zips around the corner from the storeroom, past the unisex washroom and into a cubby-hole office. Grabs the kit from off the top of the filing cabinet. Plunks it on the desk and digs out the bottle of pain reliever. Shakes out two. Finds Boots standing leaning against the counter with her back to it, rubbing her cheek.

"Here you go. Is that your Pepsi by the cash?"

"Yeah, it is. Thank you Biscuits. I think one will do. It's starting to go a little numb. Damn."

While Boots downs the pill with her drink and pockets the other, Biscuits scoots back to where she set the box down and locks the front door.

"I need to show you something. I'm sooooo excited."

Removing a folded newspaper from the top, she turns to Boots who clears a space on the counter. Unfolding the paper and removing the first section, she opens section two for the local news, and lays it out. It's dated April 17th, 1969. The photo takes the top quarter of the page and the story accompanying it is the bottom quarter. They stare at the photo with eyes aglow.

They are standing in front of their store. It is the last glassed section of a mini mall. Brown paper covers the two wide windows and door inside. Outside, tempting notices of Saturday's Opening are posted. The ladies are directly under a long, narrow sign over the door which says Two Bees Curios & Collectables. On one side of the letters is a detailed bee, floating in a bouquet of wildflowers, on the other is a peace sign made of flowers.

Boots has on a pink paisley dress that ignores the mid-thigh style, creeping upward. A frill of looped ribbon circles the hem, a deeper pink which matches a wide belt circling her slim waist. The ever-present white boots. Her wavy hair frames an oval face. Her friends tease her when she smiles and says she looks like Goldie Hawn. Biscuits is wearing plaid, wide leg slacks flared at the bottom with wide cuffs. A beige turtleneck with an orange and brown streaked scarf around her neck. Short straight hair with bangs to flatter her wide forehead. Long envious eyelashes and full natural brows are as black as her raven hair. Their smiles are on high beams.

"Look at us, Boots. You look fantastic as usual, and I look so dumpy."

"You do not look dumpy. There are a lot of women who are jealous of your curves. There doesn't seem to be any shortage of guys interested in them either. Let's read what it says."

The story tells of two women who have been friends for thirty years, since primary school. Their childhood daydreams become a reality this weekend, three days away. A friendly and equal collaboration between Charlotte DesRoches (aka Boots) and Marla Coffey (aka Biscuits). DesRoches leaves a nursing career to pursue her desire to be a business owner surrounded by things she loves, antiques, curiosities, and rare collections. Coffey was the recent owner of Coffey's Bakery, famous for her biscuits. She regards this venture as a timely opportunity and needed a change from the long hours the bakery required. Working alongside her lifelong friend is a plus too. The reporter gives them a chance for a sales pitch, and each proclaims the quality, fair prices, and mystery at Two Bees.

Biscuits is a fast reader and stands straighter. Backs away from the counter so Boots can look closer.

"That short dress you're wearing, Boots, should bring in a few hundred males. Hope they bring their wallets. Damn it girl, wish I had those legs."

"Yeah? Well, I wish I had those gorgeous eyebrows of yours. Mine are so light if I didn't pencil them in, they'd disappear."

"It is what it is, right sister?"

Boots looks back at the mess on the storeroom floor, her arms akimbo.

"I'm going to start cleaning that up. Sorry I was so clumsy. Hate to see the wine glasses go. Then we need to finish setting up the bookcases and sorting out the books before we do a final cleaning for Saturday."

"Yeah, and we need to go through and finish pricing the last four boxes we bought at the auction last Sunday. Later today, Scott is bringing the cabinet he refinished for the salt and pepper shakers. We owe him twenty dollars, and we can do it out of the petty cash. Tomorrow we put out the flyers. Then Friday, a full sweep and dusting. Yahoo!"

Her shriek causes Boots to jump back, alarmed by Biscuits' sudden gush of joy. Forgetting her sore forehead, she joins in the revelry. At the top of her lungs.

"Yahoooooooooo!"

Biscuits too starts yelping and the girls are dancing around the floor. The hoots and echoes are loud enough to be heard outdoors. Drifting shoppers pause and wonder what the commotion is about. The ladies whoop it along and laugh at each other for a few minutes until Biscuits pushes her friend away.

"It's going to be fun, Boots. Let's go grab a coffee before we get started. It's almost nine and the early crowd will have gone."

"Ok. And a double chocolate donut, too. And maybe an apple fritter. And a ..."

Biscuits looks at Boot's waist and shakes her head, can't understand how it never changes, no matter what she eats.

"I don't get it. I gain weight from looking at the damn things and you stuff your face and never change."

They lock up, and last-minute things for Saturday's opening dominate their conversation.

It's a perfect spring day. A beautiful cloudless sky graces the morning. Dandelions with their yellow faces are spread along the path Biscuits takes to the store. Robins peck at the grass and pull wriggly worms from the soil. Chickadees flitter through the trees searching for insects and seeds. The trail rambles through the park to the back of the mall property. She's the first to arrive. By six-thirty she has the brown paper torn off from inside the windows and is outside shining the glass when Boots shows up. The sun is beginning its rise behind the store and the overhang makes a comfortable shadow in the front. The weatherman is calling for a high of seventy-two degrees with a chance of rain later in the evening. Perfect for their opening.

Boots is wearing new white bell-bottoms, which show off her long legs. A black sleeveless top and a knotted scarf of black and white polka dots make up her ensemble. Hair in a ponytail and shiny white boots, of course. She's carrying her usual tote, all sparkles with faux gemstones around the top. It could hold a week's worth of groceries easily. She also carries two takeout cups of coffee. Biscuits finishes polishing the glass on the door when Boots approaches.

"Good morning, Biscuits. Isn't it a gorgeous day?"

"Good morning to you, too. Did you remember to bring the cash float?"

"Un huh. Plus, the cash reserve I picked up at the bank yesterday.

We'll put it in the safe. I hate carrying this much around."

"Yes, for sure. Love the outfit."

"Well, I love yours too. Never seen you in anything quite so daring before."

Biscuits looks down at her outfit. The Khaki bell-bottoms with ecru stripes hang low on her ample hips. A dark blue blouse is tucked in, wide white collar open to expose a teasing view of cleavage. She left her hair intentionally disarrayed on the top, tired of being accused of not taking risks.

"Well, thank you. Think there's too much boobs showing?"

"Humph. If I had those puppies, I'd be showing them off too. Nah, you look great and I like your hair. Here's your coffee. Let me get settled and ready for eight."

The last thing Boots does is swirl a bowl of fresh potpourri with a lavender scent around the store before settling it near the cash. At seven-fifty there is a line-up outside the store. Curious faces lean close, open palm over their eyes. They look in their shadow trying to see in. Biscuits does a last swipe on the counter, which is on the left when you enter; an eight-foot rectangle of polished wood. Cash register on one end, Chargex machine and forms beside it. Serving area and impulse items take up the rest. Boots is straightening her scarf and from a drawer behind the counter, removes a compact mirror and her favorite lipstick, Coral Nights, and touches up the edges. Liking what she sees, she snaps the mirror shut, tosses them both back in the drawer.

"Ok, my friend. Bring them on!"

Biscuits returns the polishing cloth to its shelf behind the counter. She turns to give Boots a hug. Her smile couldn't be any brighter.

"This is it, Boots. And look at the people waiting to get in. So, like we said, we get busy, I'll run the cash, you do the selling. You're so much better at it than me."

"I'm happy to. You get along better with numbers than I do anyway. Ready?"

"Yep! Let's do it."

They go to the door; Biscuits unlocks it and swings it opens. Standing side by side, they greet the first guests.

"Welcome to Two Bees. We're never too busy for you."

Standing aside with nervous jitters, they're amazed at the onrush of the twenty or so people waiting to get in. They look at each other with satisfied relief as the women start 'oohing' and exclaiming delight at the collections. The shoppers spread out and go into low gear, admiring, touching, sitting in some of the chairs, looking at price tags. The store has been divided into themes. Everything in each setting is for sale. A living room, a dining area, a bedroom, a kitchen. A section for the men with tools and car gadgets. Knick knacks clutter each open space and cover every surface. Art and prints hang on the walls. Bookshelves on the back right wall. Tables along the front window opposite the cash area hold an eclectic array of antiques, one dedicated to toys and dolls.

Biscuits is being asked about a rocking chair by two ladies who must be sisters, such large ears amongst friends could not be coincidental even if the same haircut was. Boots ventures in, starting with a young couple at the cabinet with salt and pepper shakers displayed. They've been eyeing them for a while.

"Hi. Did you have any questions? Can I be of help?"

The couple end up with one of Boots' favorites. The shakers are miniature slices of bread, one white, the other black and they fit inside a chrome-like toaster about the size of an orange. Plastic, but quite rare. They also take the small ceramic Dutch boy and girl. Boots discovers they're on their honeymoon, on their way to Cape Breton. The bride wants to start her own collection. Saw the ad in the newspaper.

Biscuits helps the ladies get the rocking chair into the trunk of their car. They *are* sisters. Rushes back inside to find a lineup at the cash register with Boots looking flustered. She'd prefer to be working the crowd. Biscuits is in love with numbers and doesn't need a calculator most times and takes over. She's awed by the sales and hopes it keeps going but inside she knows this is the opening and things will settle down, but it's a good sign. She serves them with a genuine smile and is profuse with her thank yous.

Some people leave without finding anything of interest, but most people buy. The morning passes swiftly, each covering the base when nature calls, both dying for a cup of coffee. It's shortly after eleven when they catch their first lull. The only customers are an elderly couple, bundled in matching cardigans regardless of the warm weather, who said they only want to look. Same for two teenage girls. Just looking. Boots joins her partner at the counter.

"That went well so far, didn't it? How're we doing?"

Biscuits can't hold back her glee and her face splits in the happiest of smiles.

"Eight hundred and forty-six dollars and fifty-five cents, to be exact."

Boots offers her friend a pat on the back and a whoop, but not too loud. Loud enough for both couples to stop and stare. The teenagers with hands over their mouths, giggling. The older couple frowns.

"Way better than we thought, huh? And I think that couple with the baby might take the couch, said they'd be back. I could see in her eyes she wanted it, but he says we're charging too much. I reminded him of it being a classic design from the early fifties and in mint condition. Offered him ten dollars off if he wanted to arrange delivery. That's what we pay Filmore's Trucking for delivering, so we don't lose anything."

"Good sales pitch and—"

They're interrupted when a boy enters the store. He has a brown paper bag in one hand, his grip tight on the rolled top. Long hair tucked behind his ears, the eyes dart everywhere. His jeans are too short, and the knees are smudged. The red tee shirt has a torn collar, but it looks clean. He approaches them, and holding the bag in front with both hands, he addresses Boots. She has to lean close to hear him.

"Excuse me ma'am. Is this a pawn shop? Do you buy things?"

She guesses him to be the same age as her nephew Jessie, twelve. Maybe eleven.

"We're kind of like a pawn shop but we don't lend money if that's what you're looking for. We do buy things if what you have to offer is unique."

She notices his confused look at "unique".

"If it's different, we might be interested."

She points at the bag he's clutching.

"What do you have?"

Unrolling the tissue, soft from much handling, he reaches in and removes a gun. He's holding it fingertips around the barrel, the handgrip hanging down. If it went off now, it would blow a hole through his palm. It doesn't matter how he's holding it; all anyone sees is a gun. The women jump back. The teenagers drop to the floor. The elderly couple makes for the door. Biscuits ducks behind the counter. Boots is waving at him, backing away.

"Put that down. You can have our money. Don't hurt anybody."

The boy's eyes go wide, and he drops the gun on the counter and steps back.

"No, no ... I only want to sell the gun. I'm not robbing you. It's not even loaded."

The teenagers are watching, have risen from the floor. The sight of the gun stirs their curiosity. Boots holds a hand to her chest wanting her heart to slow down. Biscuits is peering over the counter, her eyes level with the top. Spying the gun, she stares at it as she straightens her back.

"I don't think we buy guns; do we Boots? Where did you get this, young man?"

"It belongs to my father."

"Why didn't he bring it himself?"

"He's in a wheelchair and doesn't get around good."

Boots soaks it in right away, feeling pity. Doesn't see any deviousness in the drawn face. Biscuits is more of cynical, not as gullible.

"How do we know you didn't steal it?"

The boy shrugs and looks down at his feet.

"You don't. Only my word."

Biscuits feels bad for the boy, convinced it is his father's, but it's illegal for them to buy weapons.

"I'm sorry but it's against the law for us to buy guns."

The boy looks up and the dark eyes are pools, a lost look. He reaches for the gun and puts it back in the bag.

"Please. We don't have any food at home. Just five dollars."

Boots, who is almost in tears, goes to the locked drawer behind the counter and opens it to remove a twenty-dollar bill from the petty cash box. Glancing at Biscuits who looks askance, she says, "I'll replace this later."

She gives the boy the money as she guides him from the store. Telling him to take the gun home and get some food, and to please not bring it back. She follows three ladies who enter the store as Biscuits greets them. She steps aside as the teenagers leave, but not before they say how rad it was to see a real gun. When they're gone, she bends to Biscuits ear.

"That scared me."

"Damn, me too."

"I don't want anything else to do with people selling guns."

The rest of the afternoon is filled with curious and serious shoppers. The girls net another five hundred and sixteen dollars and thirty-eight cents when Biscuits removes the extra cash from the register and is placing it in the safe at five-thirty, a half hour before closing. There is no one in the store when Biscuits is in the back office and Boots is tidying the counter. A man walks in and goes up to Boots. She greets him with her killer smile, hoping for one more sale to complete her day.

He is wearing a cardigan which has seen better days. He needs a shave, and a haircut is what Boots is thinking. She's about to ask him if she can help when he takes a gun from the pocket of his cardigan. He's standing too close to his victim. Pointing it at Boots he opens his mouth to say something. Boots thinks it's another person wanting to sell a gun.

She reacts instantly, grabbing it by the barrel and swiping it from his hand, about to scold him. He's dumbfounded and can't even speak, stunned by the woman's swift action. She's holding it in her palm and about to tell him they don't buy guns when her finger strikes the trigger. Bam! Behind her, the glass from a framed picture of two horses running on the beach shatters, shards shoot out like needles. The man drops to the floor. Startled by the noise and the fact it's loaded; Boots screams and fumbles with the gun. Biscuits comes running from the backroom. The man's head darts back and forth, unprepared for the turn of events, rises and runs for the door. Boots loses her grip on the weapon, and it falls on the floor. The impact causes it to fire again. The bullet shatters the culprit's right Achilles tendon, bursts a valuable Rovenstyn nineteenth century urn, disappearing into the wall. The man is propelled forward. He slams his head on the glass door. Crashes to the floor. Biscuits is screaming, shaking her hands in the air, thinking the man is dead. Boots is already on the phone to 911.

"Stay cool Biscuits."

The line connects, and even though her heart is pounding, Boots remains calm and explains the situation.

"...111 Belvedere Drive in the north end, the Morningside Mall. Suite 12, last on the left from the main entrance. Hurry."

Biscuits is standing by the counter, her eyes glued to the bleeding foot, the unconscious man. She holds her face in both hands and closes her eyes, trying to blot everything out.

Boots gets her hands under the man's shoulders and drags him aside, away from the door. People are gathering outside. She tells Biscuits not to touch the damn gun. Not even five minutes go by when a police officer pushes the crowd aside, and another enters the store. With gun drawn, she points it at the two Bees, who, wide-eyed, shoot their hands in the air and stare at the officer.

"I'm Officer Loretta Gibbs. What happened here?"

Biscuits is too tense to speak, but Boots steps forward, her chin out, pointing to the pistol lying on the floor.

"He pulled a gun on us. It's there on the floor."

Seeing the inert man, she bends to check for a pulse and his breathing. Finding both, she sees the damaged sneaker and a grey sock turning burgundy along the edge. She inspects the wound. The man is in a supine position from when Boots pulled him away. She turns to the woman, keeping the man in her peripheral vision then looks down at the man with a glint in her eyes.

"Seems he picked the wrong day. Relax, but stick close. The ambulance is on the way. I can hear the siren now. I'm going to cuff this guy. Then we need a statement from you. My partner will do that as soon as he clears the crowd outside. Sit tight, ladies."

Two and a half hours later, Boots locks the store door, turns and leans back on it, brushing the stray hairs from her face. A heavy sigh escapes her lips, disbelief shading her eyes. Looking at her friend who is sprawled in one of the office chairs moved to the counter, spinning it back and forth, a faraway look on her face.

"Thank goodness that's over."

"Yes, yes, yes ... I'm exhausted. Oh damn, Boots, I never want to see another gun as long as I live."

"I know I never want to touch one again. Can you imagine the odds of that happening. Two guns in one day. Three if you count Officer Gibbs. The first day we're open for business."

Biscuits pushes herself up from the chair and stands near Boots. Her hands on her hips. She looks like she's trying not to laugh.

"Think about it for a minute ... you could've shot the guy. All that fuss over his messed-up heel, he comes to rob us, and they hang a guilt trip on you for being careless with the gun. If you'd put a bullet through him by mistake, we'd be doing an all-nighter and you would've ruined everybody's day. Can you believe it?"

Boots shivers at the very idea and pouts. Biscuits can't hold it in, the whole absurdity of guns and ambulances and the police, the fear, the shock, the scruffy crook ... she's laughing so hard, she has to lean against the counter. She has a quiet, shoulder shaking laugh, a few snickers, the eyes laughing too. The hilarity hits Boots like a flood and drains the stress away. With their backs to the counter, they laugh until their stomachs hurt. They wear it out, down to catching their breath and both turn quiet. Boots puts her arms around her pal's shoulder.

"C'mon my friend, let's go home. Tomorrow is a new day. It can't get any worse."

Allan Hudson

Growing up in South Branch, Allan Hudson was encouraged to read from an early age by his mother who was a schoolteacher. He lives in Dieppe, NB, with his wife Gloria. He has enjoyed a lifetime of adventure, travel and uses the many experiences as ideas for his writing. He is an author of action/adventure novels, historical fiction and a short story collection. His short stories – The Ship Breakers & In the Abyss – received Honorable Mention in the New Brunswick Writer's Federation competition.

He has stories published on commuterlit.com, The Golden Ratio and his blog - South Branch Scribbler.

www.southbranchscribbler.ca

Love and Crafts

By Angella Cormier

THE LAST FEW DAYS OF WINTER had left the wharf in complete disarray. The snow was melting fast since spring had made its arrival on the southern shores of New Brunswick. This area, like several others in the coastal regions of the province, was beginning to buzz with activity in anticipation of warmer days to come. Summer would soon be upon the residents and the many tourists who came to visit the small town of Larton.

Estelle had made her way from the nearby city of Holk to the neighboring coastal town in her little grey Toyota Yaris. She had named her car Getty, out of her love for the actress that bore the same first name as her in the popular series with the four old women living under the same roof. Single and living alone, she watched at least one episode of the *Golden Girls* every night before bed. The witty jokes of the comical sitcom helped Estelle keep loneliness at bay. In her early sixties, with only one grown daughter living across the world in Australia with a family of her own, Estelle tried her best to keep busy with hobbies and freelance work as a bookkeeper.

Today Estelle was on one of her weekly adventures. Earlier that morning, she had packed up a few items she would need for the short trip. In her backpack were her binoculars, her small point-and-shoot camera, her notepad and a pen. She also kept a cooler-lined lunch bag and water bottle in her car, as these adventures, though never fully planned out, usually kept her away from the house on weekends, for full days at length.

Birdwatching had become her favorite hobby, if not her passion.

She often watched the window in her home office when the movement of fluttering wings or the song of a feathered friend captured her attention. She had become accustomed to writing down the time, date and place, as well as the bird type, its gender and what it was doing when spotted. She would summarize all the information at the end of each week and report these findings to the online portal at eBird.org. The website would then compile these findings, in order to contribute to certain conservation decisions and towards bird research worldwide. She held a fascination and a love for birds that was unparalleled to her other hobbies; knitting, cooking pastries and learning to play the ukelele were just not as much fun for this free-spirited gal. She loved being outdoors and the never-ending hunt to spot new bird species kept her on her toes, both figuratively and literally.

Estelle shifted the Yaris into park and scanned the view of the wharf and nearby marina. No boats were yet docked in the frigid water. The large wall of rocks that had been formed in the water by Larton's Wharf Authority was covered in a thin layer of white foam, no doubt freezing in the overnight hours, but melting during the warmer days of April. The sun shone bright today, which made Estelle happy. The winter had been long.

Grabbing her backpack, she exited her car, locked the doors and headed towards the edge of the wharf. Her excitement waned when she noticed a few other parked vehicles. Inside each of these, teenagers were conversing and laughing above the loud rap music that echoed from one of the cars. The base would be so loud in some songs that she could feel the vibrations in her chest, even from this distance.

"*That won't attract birds.*" she thought as she walked further away from the youngsters. She made her way to the edge of the wharf, where large concrete barriers had been placed decades prior to safeguard cars from going over the edge and into the deep waters below. She noticed two seagulls on the rocks, their plumage ruffling in the light wind. The sun shone bright on them, showing off their plump bellies, likely full of discarded french fries from the local *McDonald's*.

Estelle opened her backpack to retrieve her camera. She snapped a few quick photos of the winged-rats and scribbled the count into her notepad. "*It's a start.*" she reasoned. As common as they were, they were still important to track, just as much as any other bird. She put the items back in her backpack and decided the sun was warm enough to take off her fleece jacket she had worn until now. She wrapped the jacket around her waist and put the backpack back on.

Looking down at the water, she admired the sparkling reflection of the sky dancing up and down on the soft waves as they gently slapped the side of the wharf. Memories of her childhood rushed back, to a time when her parents brought her and her siblings swimming in the lake. There had been a wooden dock there, the sound of the waves created a similar flow echoing through her mind. Her memories drifted back; her eyes focused on the soft rhythmic flow that lulled her into a calm state.

With her thoughts lost in long past childhood memories, she did not notice the old man on the bicycle approaching her from behind.

Estelle felt a cold hand on her bare shoulder. She jumped from the unexpected touch and turned instantly to come face to face with an older gentleman. He was sitting on an old ten speed CCM bicycle that looked like it had seen better days. The man rolled back a few feet; he seemed suddenly aware he had caught her by surprise or worse, that he had scared her. When he opened his mouth to speak, Estelle noticed he had several teeth missing. The scruff on his chin was more than likely because he did not have a home, or that he just didn't care enough to keep himself presentable. He showed her a nervous smile, placed his hand back on the handlebar of his bike and spoke with a soft but raspy voice. She concluded this would be from years of smoking, based on the scent of tobacco that wafted her way.

"Sorry, so sorry. I didn't mean to scare you. " His apology seemed sincere, but Estelle kept her guard up. She didn't just automatically trust people, especially not those who came up to her out of nowhere, like this gentleman had done.

"It's okay. Is there anything I can help you with?" she asked, as she took a step back, putting a bit more distance between herself and the older man.

"No, oh no. I just saw you taking pictures of the gulls, over there. Y'a know they mate for life, them?" He looked at her with wide eyes, growing excitedly as he continued, "They take turns sitting on the eggs, they do. I saw that on PBS when I had cable years ago. Years and years ago. When I had cable." Another smile to soften the initial shock of his arrival. Estelle smiled back, realizing the man seemed genuinely sincere. He also appeared a bit simple-minded, but she didn't dare assume as much. Returning a smile of her own, she softened.

"That's interesting! I didn't know that!" Estelle replied.

"And there are so many other things I saw on PBS. It was the Maine channel, and there's lots of birds there and so they had a special show. On cable, when I had it, a long time ago. I don't anymore. But I learned so much about seagulls and ducks and all kinds of birds."

Estelle realized her suspicions were accurate. He was simple-minded, but ever so fascinating with his love of birds and the Public Broadcasting Service.

"That's great to hear. I'm Estelle, by the way." She stepped a bit closer to the man on the bicycle and extended her hand. A simple but warm gesture to show him that she wasn't upset or scared. "What's your name?" she asked with a smile.

"Oh, that's not important. But if you have to know, it's Earl. Earl without the E at the end. That's what my momma always said and so now I say that, too." His eyes shot downwards for a moment, and a flash of sadness spread across his face. "She isn't here anymore, momma. She passed away four years ago. At least I think it's been four years. I lose track of days sometimes. But I keep busy. With the birds and the butterflies and all." His face lit up again and Estelle noticed his eyes were watery. She felt sad for the man named Earl. Earl with no E at the end, she noted mentally.

"I hope I didn't scare you, Estelle. I just wanted to tell you that I think your tattoo is cool. Very cool, if you ask me." From his oversized windbreaker, he pulled out a pair of binoculars that had been hidden from view. "I like to look at birds too, Estelle. I was looking at the island across the bay when you came into view in my bi'culars. That's when I saw your tattoo. Very cool tattoo."

Estelle, a bit surprised by his comment, asked him if he knew what it was.

"Well, I can't say for sure." Earl took off his ball cap and scratched his forehead. "Is it some kind of sea monster?" he asked. Placing his cap back on, he watched as Estelle turned a bit to show him the shoulder where her tattoo had been inked decades earlier.

"I don't know if you ever heard of it, but it's a Lovecraftian monster. It's called Cthulhu. It's kind of a sea monster, but it's more of an alien than a monster, as it came from another planet. Well in the stories, I mean. H.P. Lovecraft was a writer and in the 1920's he wrote a story titled 'The call of Cthulhu' and that's when it was invented." About fifteen seconds went by and Estelle realized Earl had no idea what she was talking about.

"Ohh, oh I see," he said hesitantly. "Never heard tell of that."

She tried to return the conversation to something he would be more interested in or knowledgeable about. She turned to face the island across the bay. Pointing towards the small, uninhabited piece of land, she asked him:

"What kind of birds do you see out there? Anything interesting?"

"Oh yeah. Yes ma'am. There are big ones. I saw an Osprey flying from the island to the wharf here just last week. It comes out when someone is fishing over here," he says while pointing across the way. "They come and try to steal some fish. Easy catch for them. Sometimes they do. Sometimes they don't." Earl stepped off his bike and used his heel to put the kickstand in place. Stepping next to Estelle, he lifted his binoculars and looked towards the East end of the isle.

"There though, on the end where the trees aren't as thick, there's some I ain't ever saw before. Huge, yup huge, but they never leave the island. I don't know what they are, 'cause they hide real good too."

Curious, Estelle took her own binoculars and set her sight on the eastern tip of the island. She scanned the view to see if she could spot and maybe figure out what Earl said he saw.

"Did they have any color to them? Any markings or something to help identify what they could be?" Her curiosity now had the best of her.

"Nah. Well a bit, but only in parts. Like I said. They hide a lot. I seen a bit of yellow once. Then another one, I think it was white. But only just part of it. The rest was behind the fence and in with the trees. Hard to see them. Huge though."

Estelle dropped her binoculars and looked at Earl.

"Fence? I didn't know there was fencing over there. Why would anyone have put up fencing?" She returned her gaze to the island through the focal point of her binoculars, searching for the fence that Earl mentioned.

"No idea, Estelle. All I know is one day, when I was looking for the Osprey and their babies, I noticed the fence there. Not sure when they put it up."

"Who are *they*, Earl?"

"Not sure, but they only go at night. Sometimes I come here late at night to look at the stars, there. Momma used to do that with us when we were kids. And so, when I do it now, I think of momma and my brother Elmo."

Estelle realized she might not get much of an answer but pressed on.

"Okay, so they go at night-time. What do they look like? Men? Women? How many of them?"

"Oh, well that's hard to say. Cause all I ever see is the flashlight. They just walk around and shine a light here and there. I don't know how they got there either. Never seen anyone going over there except the summer tourists who go on the Bay Tour with Ralph. But Ralph doesn't stop on the island, he just goes around there and back. Maybe Ralph knows."

Estelle put a hand on the man's shoulder. "Thanks Earl. It's a pleasure having met you. I'm sure we will see more of each other this spring and summer. You have me curious now." She smiled wide as a light cool breeze made her long gray hair cover part of her face.

"Nice to meet you too, Estelle." Tipping his cap her way, he set down the pair of binoculars and reached into his windbreaker pocket, from which he took out rolling paper and a tobacco pouch. "I gotta go now. Can't afford to lose any of this in the wind." He motioned to the pouch.

"Alright, Earl. You have a great day." She watched him sit on his bicycle again and kick the stand into place before he put his feet to the pedals. "Wait! Earl," she called out before he was too far. Earl braked and turned his head around, waiting for her to finish. "How about we meet back here next week. Same place, same time on Saturday. We can try to figure out what it was you saw and who *they* are."

Earl grinned, flashing more gums than teeth, but a genuine smile it was.

"That would be really nice, Estelle. I'll be here." Off he went towards the marina, where the building blocked the wind.

That evening, Estelle couldn't stop thinking about what Earl had told her he'd seen on the island. She had stayed for about an hour after he'd left. She had watched that side of the island intently but had not seen much of anything bird-wise. She did, however, spot the fencing. It was very difficult to make out against the foliage this time of year. The only reason she did see it was due to a small 'NO TRESPASSING' sign that had been placed on it. She had spotted that first and after focusing around that area, she had seen the fence. *Why would there be a fence on the island, though,* she pondered.

She poured a cup of Earl Gray tea and sat with her iPad in the living room. She searched online for any mention of the island, the fence or the large birds that Earl had spoken about. Absolutely no results found online. She went to the kitchen and poured another cup of tea, when an idea came to her.

She grabbed her keys off the kitchen table, put on her fleece jacket and nearly ran to the back door where she put on her sneakers as fast as she could. She picked up her backpack that was sitting on the floor near the door. Without thinking twice, she headed out in the darkness of night.

The temperature had dropped significantly from earlier in the day when Estelle reached the wharf. She exited her Yaris and went to the hatch where she retrieved an emergency blanket, a flashlight and her backpack.

Looking around, she was happy to see that her guess was right. The wharf was completely deserted. In another two months, the restaurant and patio bars would be open. The boaters and tourists would be on the wharf until the wee small hours. Also, there would no doubt be more teenagers looking for a spot to go parking. She knew this from her own younger years, when she was a bit wilder and loved adventures.

Quite the adventure you're going on tonight, Estelle! She smirked as she realized this was the first time in a very long time, decades even, that she had dared to do something so outlandish. For a split second she questioned if she should really go forward with her plan. As she closed the hatch to her car, she felt a surge of adrenaline come up, and instantly she knew she had to do this.

She took the items she had retrieved from the car. She wrapped the blanket around her shoulders, tying a knot in it to secure it in place around her neck. Next, the flashlight went inside her fleece pocket. Last, she slipped the straps of the backpack onto her shoulders. She hoped the plan she had hatched in but a few moments back at home would be enough to get her through this quest.

Walking in the shadows, she reached the marina. The building was dark, except for the dim solar lights that had been installed around the property. She didn't notice any video cameras on the side of the building; only one appeared near the front entrance. She assumed it was a decoy as the wharf had struggled for many years to stay afloat with repairs and renovations. Doubtful she would be caught, she continued in the shadows until she made it to the side of the building. There she spotted what she had come to retrieve.

Though covered for the winter, she had seen the small vinyl inflatable dinghy hung on the side of the building, along with two oars and an air pump last summer. She pulled the polyester tarp off the small boat and set it aside. She grabbed the dinghy and got busy inflating it to almost full capacity. Luckily this only took about five minutes. The dinghy was there for emergencies around the wharf, and so they had invested in a pump that would fill or top up the boat fast.

She was ready to set out. She threw the oars inside the inflated raft and balanced it above her head. She was surprised at how light the oars were. She walked with the eight-foot-long boat until she reached the side of the wharf, where she sauntered onto one of the dock's gangways; she took small prudent steps all the way to the end of the metal walkway until she reached the water. There, she set it down in the calm water and got in.

The trek was longer than she anticipated. Although it seemed fairly close, the kilometer or so distance from the wharf to the island made her realize how much she needed to go back to the gym for strength training.

Once she reached the eastern part of the island, she pulled the small dinghy onto shore, making sure to leave it far enough from the water so that she could make it back safely once she was done.

It took no time for her to find the fence she had spotted earlier that day in the thicket of trees, still barren of leaves.

"Let's see what is hiding behind this fence," she murmured. When she reached the sign that read 'NO TRESPASSING', she noticed there wasn't anything atop the metal cross-link fencing. She managed to climb up and over the fence, albeit with effort, she was still in decent shape after all.

The wind was a tad stronger here, more than likely because it was out in the open in the middle of the bay. She pulled the zipper of her fleece up to her chin, took out the flashlight from her pocket and walked into the woods.

The island was quiet, except for the soft waves on the shore and the wind that came and went in short-lived breezes. There seemed to be a beaten path, which she followed as best she could. *Whatever these people were doing here, they've been doing it for a while. Otherwise, this path wouldn't exist,* she thought. Earl came to mind. She would ask him how many times he had spotted them.

From a short distance, there came a fluttering noise. It sounded like wings, but it was too loud for that. It whooshed nearby. Estelle moved her flashlight and tried to pinpoint its source. She held her breath as it resonated again, this time very close to her. She distinguished it was coming from above her, and not around her. Shining the beam of light upwards, she caught quick movement out of the corner of her eye. A white or yellow wing, it seemed. A large wing, much too large to be believable. Earl had not made up what he had seen. This was the biggest wing she had ever seen.

Eyes wide, she swept the beam of light from one tree to another, illuminating the leafless woods around her, trying to find the source of the sound, of the large, winged bird she had just missed. Standing stock still, she listened with anticipation for the sound to come again. After a few moments, it came, having moved further north, deeper in the wooded area. She hurried to catch up with the sound, her flashlight lighting the way. The beam of light jumped up and down as she ran. She was intent on seeing the creature that Earl had described earlier. Had it not been that the fence was up, she may not have believed the ramblings of the man. However, with the fence, hearing the fluttering and seeing a flash of the enormous wing, she could not ignore the reality of it.

She ran further into the woods until she came upon a clearing. The trees had all been cut down. The trunks remained, but the wood had been carried away. Estelle estimated the clearing was at least twenty feet in diameter. She moved towards the center of the area, listening intently to hear the fluttering noise again, or anything else that may hint at where to find the bird that made such a pronounced noise.

In the middle of the clearing, her sneaker hit something hard. Looking down, she found a metal hatch. Her foot had hit the handle. Kneeling, she pushed the debris away from the rectangular door that led to an apparent underground space below. On the metal surface, a large sticker read: 'ABSOLUTELY NO TRESPASSING'. Below the warning, in smaller letters: 'Testing Grounds of Enhancing Lepidopterology, Property of Schmetten Laboratories.' Estelle stared at the words, trying to make sense of what she was seeing. Had the island become some sort of experimental grounds? If it was, what exactly were they trying to do? She didn't know what Lepidopterology meant. It could be anything. Still kneeling, she debated whether she should take photos of this, and report it to the Town Council. *Are they aware*, she wondered, *are the residents aware?*

From above there came a soft crackling. Her eyes peered into the darkness, hoping to see it without the flashlight. She assumed the bright light might have scared it away moments prior. She could make out a shape, lighter in the darkness, however she couldn't make out what exactly it was. Slowly, she raised the flashlight towards the silhouette that seemed to be hanging from a tree.

Estelle gasped, her breath catching in her throat. Above her, on a branch, there hung the biggest cocoon she had ever seen. It shone in the light of the battery powered torch she held. From the distance between them, she couldn't see much. The crackling sound had stopped, and this cocoon thing didn't seem to move at all. Not taking her eyes off the shape in the tree, Estelle slid her backpack off her shoulders, unzipped it and took out her binoculars. With one hand she lifted the light again on the large cocoon shape and with the other she peered into the binoculars.

"What in the world?" Estelle couldn't find words to describe what she saw. It looked like a butterfly's cocoon. A shining, silk-like material was wrapped in on itself, woven in such a way as to contain whatever was inside. That was normal enough, but the sheer size of the cocoon made her mind swim in wonder. It measured at least six feet long and two feet wide.

After examining the cocoon shape for a few minutes, she decided she needed to document this discovery. Whatever this was, someone knew about it. She intended to find out who they were and what they were doing here. Kneeling on the damp forest floor, she dug out her point and shoot camera from her bag and put away the binoculars again.

Aiming to get the best angle possible, she stepped a few feet back before pressing the button. The bright flash from the camera went off, once, twice, three times. No movement, no sound came from the cocoon. On the last flash though, Estelle noticed out of the corner of her eye more shapes hanging in the trees. Grabbing the flashlight again, she spun around as she looked up. At least a dozen cocoons hung from the branches above and around her. Too stunned to think, Estelle started putting everything back in her backpack. Suddenly, she didn't want to be here anymore.

Going back onto the path from which she came, she ran with the flashlight guiding her way. The last thing she wanted was to trip and hurt herself. She did not want to be stuck on the island with these things, whatever they were. When she finally reached the fence, she threw her backpack over onto the other side, stuffed her flashlight in her fleece pocket and grabbed the chain-link with one hand. Just as she was about to put her foot on the fence to climb over, she felt something grab at it. Through her pants, it felt warm around her ankle and then climbing up her leg, the warmth spread slowly.

She looked downwards, unable to see properly. With her free

hand, she grabbed the flashlight from her fleece pocket. Struggling to turn it on with just one hand, she could feel the warm sensation at her knee now. Finally, she managed to turn on the light and shone it down on her leg.

Estelle screamed. The thing that had taken hold of her leg was as large as she was. Shaped like a caterpillar, it had no legs nor arms, but its body was covered with long fur. It slithered up her body, inch by inch.

Her scream became muffled by the sound of fluttering above her. She could feel large wings, delicate yet strong, hitting her head and her arms. Trying to defend herself, she hit it with the flashlight, but it was knocked out of her hand. It hit her so hard that she fell to the ground and onto her belly, sprawled out with her legs behind her. The flashlight on the ground, it illuminated the creature that was entwined on one of her legs completely. In the beam of light, she saw another giant caterpillar creature, this one way larger than the one around her leg, slithering its way toward her face. She felt dizzy from hyperventilating, but she tried to escape the thing that was on her. She realized that her leg no longer had any feeling. Numb from the hip down, she could not move, and it became obvious to her that she was trapped.

Dragging her body with her arms, she made her way to the fence. There, she turned and leaned her back against it, waiting for the giant creature in the darkness. She could hear the dead leaves and branches on the ground as it crept towards her. The last thing Estelle saw was the shadow of the enormous creature. It consumed her body slowly. With much effort, it stretched and elongated, until Estelle was fully devoured.

The creature, full of its feed, retracted from the open area and climbed a nearby tree, making its way back to its silken nest, where dozens more waited for prey.

The following Saturday, Earl arrived at the wharf at the same time he had the week prior. He looked forward to seeing his new friend Estelle. She had been very kind to him. Not many people were kind to him ever since his mother had passed away.

He made his way to the end of the wharf on his bicycle. There, he noticed Estelle's car. There were some police cruisers at the marina, which he thought was unusual. This time of year, nothing much happened there as it was mostly deserted until the warm weather became permanent.

"Hi officer, what's going on?" he approached the policeman, with curiosity and concern.

"Hey Earl. Seems to have been a theft during the week. We got a call from the wharf manager who came in today. The rescue inflatable raft has been taken along with the oars. The pump was left behind though." The officer pointed towards the side of the marina, where the tarp and the pump were on the ground. "Did you happen to see anyone here lately that looked out of place?"

Earl rubbed his neck with his hand. He often did this whenever he got nervous. "Well, I did see someone last Saturday. She was an awfully nice lady though. I doubt she would have stolen a thing." He nodded towards her car in the nearly empty parking lot. "We had plans to meet today. To look at the birds and stuff." Earl realized the cops likely didn't believe him. He noticed how they had glanced at each other. Their faces had grimaced just enough for him to know that they weren't buying it.

"It's true. She even said she would help me figure out what's on the island over there." Turning his bicycle around to face the island, he pedaled slowly a few feet away. "Come on, I'll show you." The officers looked at each other and decided to follow along. When they reached the edge of the wharf, they noticed Earl had a pair of binoculars in his hands. He took them off from around his neck and gave them to one of the cops. "Look, see that fence? We were going to try to figure out why it was there. And who are *they*? Estelle wanted to know who *they* were. I don't know who they are, but she seemed really serious in wanting to find out."

Confused, the officers tried to follow Earl's story. The officer brought the binoculars to his eyes and peered at the island from across the bay. His partner walked over to the Yaris that was parked in the lot. He cupped his hands to have a better look inside. "And this Estelle lady, did she have a last name, Earl?" He went around and looked in the hatch.

"Well, no, I mean, yes, she has a last name. But I don't know what it is. Never asked and she never said." Earl sat back on his seat and crossed his arms on his chest.

"Umm, Carl, you should see this." The officer, still holding the binoculars up to his eyes, waved his partner over with one hand.

"What? A murder of crows or is it a flock of flying rats?" Chuckling, he walked over to where his partner Joe stood staring in the plastic instrument.

"Seriously, Carl. I think we need to get over there. The raft is on the shore over there."

Earl stood up and watched as the officers called for backup.

The day became a flurry of activity on the wharf. Earl stayed, watching with his binoculars from the mainland as the police made their way to the island with the help of the coast guard. He watched as dozens of large white items were taken one by one by boat to the wharf. Most were empty, large silken wraps of some sort.

When the last one was brought to the wharf though, he knew this one was different. It was full, still intact. Whatever bird had made its home on the island, he was determined to find out. He looked around for Estelle, hoping she would show up so they could see it together. When he realized she wasn't coming, he pedaled over to the gangway to meet up with the officers.

"You shouldn't be here, Earl. We don't know what this is."

"If it wasn't for me, you wouldn't be here either, Carl." Earl stated dryly.

"Fine then, stay. But if you get sick or something, don't blame us."

Carl and Joe carried the large cocoon-like thing onto the wharf. They got the tarp from across the way and spread it out. They carefully placed the white cocoon on it. As soon as it was placed on the tarp, a crackling noise came from it. Everyone took a step or two back, unsure what to expect. They watched as the silk-like fibers began to move. Whatever was inside, it was alive.

"Careful, we don't know what this is! Let's all stay cool, okay?" Carl, obviously nervous, tried to hide this fact by commenting. He and Joe took their guns from their holsters. The coast guards stood around, waiting to help if needed. Earl watched with his mouth hanging open, waiting to finally see what it was he had spotted only quick glimpses of in recent weeks.

As the silk grew weaker, the crackling noises dissipated. The movements became stronger until there protruded a long wing from the first freshly made openings of the cocoon. Stretching itself outwardly, the creature soon escaped its natural entrapment.

"Holy mother of all that's holy. What is that?!" Carl exclaimed.

Earl looked carefully at the winged creature on the tarp as it outstretched its large wings, slowly gaining strength with each movement.

As the others watched in horror and shock, Earl came down to his knees and bent down closer to the creature.

"Do you see this? Do you know what that is?" he exclaimed; his eyes wide, he started to laugh as the others watched.

The creature managed to flap its wings; they measured a good four feet wide on each side. Its beady eyes looked into Earl's. The officers took their stance, ready to shoot if they felt they had to protect themselves or others. Earl smiled.

"EARL, back away, NOW!"

Not listening to Carl, Earl pointed to the black markings on the left wing of the creature.

"That," he pointed to the markings, "that there is Love and Crafts. See how it looks like an alien monster? Estelle told me when she showed me her tattoo. She said it was an old book or something."

The officers looked at each other again, with another glance of pity and worry. He knew they didn't understand. He tried so hard to remember what Estelle had said.

"It was in the 20's. He was a book writer and made a crew or tule. Ahhh ha! Ha! Ha!" Earl laughed so loud it took the cops by surprise.

Earl watched as the winged creature stared back at him. He knew now what the creatures were. He stood up again as the large butterfly began flapping its wings faster and faster. His eyes teared up as he tipped his cap towards the giant butterfly.

"It was great meeting you!" he called out as it flew off, over the bay heading to the island. "I won't forget you! Come back anytime and I'll tell you everything I learned on PBS, from back when I had cable."

The group of men stared at Earl, then at the creature, then back at Earl.

"What are we going to do with you, Earl?" Joe said with a worried look on his face. "And what are we going to put in our report, Carl?" He gave the binoculars back to a smiling Earl.

Everyone stared at the creature flying away. When it reached the island, it swooped downwards into the woods. For a brief moment it was no longer visible. "I have no idea, Joe. I have no freakin' idea."

Still facing the island, they all watched as a large group of twenty or so giant butterflies flew up high in the sky. Joe turned to one of the coast guard agents.

"Did you guys manage to contact Schmetten Laboratories?"

"All the numbers our admin was able to find have been disconnected, sir. Their website is offline too. It looks like they're no longer operational."

As officers Joe and Carl spoke with the coast guards, Earl got on his ten-speed bicycle and pedaled away.

"Butterflies. That was one of the PBS specials too. Yup. I remember that now, from the cable."

His voice drifted away, carried with the soft spring breeze.

Angella Cormier

Angella Cormier grew up in Saint Antoine, a small town in south east New Brunswick, Canada. This is where her love of reading and writing was born. Her curious nature about everything mysterious and paranormal helped carve the inspiration for her passion of writing horror and mystery stories. She is also a published poet, balancing out her writing to express herself in these two very opposing genres.

Previous titles include: Oakwood Island - The Awakening (2020), Oakwood Island (2016), A Maiden's Perception - A collection of thoughts, reflections and poetry (2015) and Dark Tales for Dark Nights (2013, written as Angella Jacob).

www.mysteriousink.ca

Spring

Paths

✳

Thank you, dear Reader, for reaching this page.

It means that you have valiantly worked your way through all of our stories. I hope you enjoyed them as much as myself, and my fellow writers in Canada, enjoyed creating them.

I'm often asked, what it is that I particularly like about the process of writing. My answer is always short. Everything. Creating a short story or a novel is the same for me – I think a lot, I type a lot and then I submit the piece for editing and publishing. At that point, the story/book ceases to be mine. It then becomes the property of you, the Reader.

So, thank you for buying this miscellany of stories. I hope the different worlds and voices encompassed between these endpapers have kept you absorbed. I hope they have brought you enjoyment and perhaps an inkling to try one of our longer stories. If so, thank you and perhaps you might consider giving this little book a review. It doesn't have to be anything fancy or long, just a like and a rating and maybe a nod to a friend or two about why you enjoyed the stories.

And finally, I must say thank you to my fellow writers involved in this venture. Great to know you and work with you despite the distance!

Angela Wren

Did you enjoy Spring Paths?

Check out these other titles:

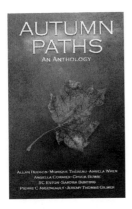

Printed in Great Britain
by Amazon

29435518R00110